The Muted Swan

F'd Up Fairy Tales

By

Michel Prince

The Muted Swan

This is a work of fiction. Names, characters, places and incidents are either the product of the author's imagination or used fictitiously, and any resemblance to actual persons, living or dead, business establishments, events or locales is entirely coincidental.

ALL RIGHTS RESERVED. No part of this book may be reproduced or transmitted in any form or by any means, electronic or mechanical, including photocopying, recording, or by an information storage and retrieval system-except by a reviewer who may quote brief passages in a review to be printed in a magazine, newspaper, or on the web -without permission in writing from the author.

EDITED BY: LEANORE ELLIOTT

Book Interior Design By: Wicked Muse

Cover Art By: Dusk Til Dawn Designs

Photo Credit
Royal Touch Photography

The Muted Swan

An F'd Up Fairytale

Copyright © 2017 Michel Prince

Michel Prince

DEDICATION

The greatest part of being a member of the interracial romance genre is meeting some amazing authors. This collaboration of fairytales were inspired by them and brought to life from my favorite movie when I was a child. The weekend runs to the video store when it was new, garnered me a trip to a magical place where The Wild Swans told a story of a sister's love for her family. As the youngest of six, the idea captured me each time I watched.

Muted Swan

Once upon a time, Elsa Swanson lived a charmed life, tucked away with her six brothers. When her father remarries, the children are thrilled to meet their stepmother. That is until they discover witches do exist in the world. A curse took her brothers from her and she must knit nettles into sweaters without making a sound until all are complete.

Duke King is a med student with an empire being handed to him. When his father chooses to extend their property to an untouched forest, they discover a woman living alone who only communicates with her eyes and gentle touches. The aspiring doctor first sees a patient, but as each day passes, he falls in love with the determined woman.

Elsa had forgotten the touch of another and had never known the feel of a man. So close to saving her brothers, the witch has returned now and is using manipulation to make Duke question Elsa's sanity. Can Elsa stay true to her brothers or will her growing desires to know Duke cause her to break her vows?

PROLOGUE

Zelda watched with two flutes of champagne in her hands, as the newly widowed Earl Swanson stood steadfast on the balcony. The glittering lights of the city twinkled as the edge of the night draped the horizon in darkness. She watched as he braced his hands on the cement railing, curling his fingers around the edge and leaning forward.

"It would be a shame to destroy such a nice tuxedo," Zelda purred. "Then again, you'd spend eternity ready for a party."

Earl stepped back from the railing. "I wasn't thinking about jumping." His voice was deep and full of the pain she could feel, yet had no ability to relate. "Just taking in the city."

"They are celebrating you in there, aren't they?" she asked stepping closer and hitching her thumb toward the patio door. "Or at least, your generous donation."

"My wife's charity," he confessed clenching his strong jaw and shaking his head. His thick blond hair just long enough to curl a bit on the end moving with his motions. "I feel a bit lost without her guiding me around the room."

All the news sources documented his wife's passing. Those in society considered the Swanson's to be royalty in the city. Their estate had been built over a hundred years ago, when the family of railroad barons finally settled down with their millions. Now, Earl lived off of investments and spent most of his evenings at charity events giving back.

"You handled these events when you were younger without being lost," Zelda mused and passed him a glass of champagne. Tiny bubbles still floated to the surface unfazed by the powder her mother gave her to win his heart. Years of training and honing her talents aside, sometimes a girl just needed her mommy for important things. Not that the skilled witch thought she couldn't win him on beauty and charm alone, but that would take time and Zelda was not known for her patience.

"Then I had my parents. Now, it's just me." He scanned the skyline again and took a sip of the drink. "And my children of course, but I would never subject them to this."

"Children?" she questioned not remembering any mention of children when she saw the papers splashed with tales of his woes.

"We kept them hidden for the most part. Tucked away. My wife was a bit paranoid of kidnapping and ransom requests. I tried to tell her we didn't live in Mexico City, but she loved a good mystery novel and I loved—" halting his words, he downed the rest of the golden liquid.

Zelda turned her eyes away to hide her pleasure in tricking the man.

Nothing better than a wealthy man on the rebound. Especially, with cool crystal blue eyes and a firm body sure to bring her at least a modicum of pleasure. It was the children she worried about. Maybe two, she could handle if necessary.

Earl's hand came into view as he placed a finger under her chin and turned it upward. A strange look danced in his eyes. "I loved my wife, but she is gone now. I did think of jumping. You saved me. Tell me your name."

"Zelda."

"Zelda," he cooed a bit as her name danced on his tongue. "What would I have to do for you to ferry me around this party and keep me from getting lost in my grief?"

"Marry me tomorrow," she teased a bit, but knew he would only be highly suggestible for the next twenty-four hours unless she could give him another dose of her mother's concoction.

"An even trade, for you seem like a woman who could keep my home and body warm."

"That I could."

The evening turned into Zelda's night. People fawned over her and women cut jealous stares at the new woman on Earl Swanson's arm.

She had arrived and by noon the next day, they were wed.

"My beautiful bride, I will be going to see my children to tell them all about you," Earl beamed as he held her in his arms why they lay naked in their marital bed. "When I return, we shall go on an extended honeymoon and then start our life together."

"Go to your children?" she asked. "Are they not somewhere on the estate?"

"I told you of their mother's worry for their safety." He cupped her cheek and laid a gentle kiss on her lips.

She wrapped her leg around his waist as the sheet tangled and tightened heightening her awareness of their naked bodies.

"She hid them away and had them tutored through online courses."

"Don't they get lonely?"

"Maybe Elsa on occasion, being the only girl, but her six brothers keep her on her toes."

What Zelda had for a heart clenched. "Seven." She smiled broadly hoping to hide her distain. "You have seven children?"

"Yes, and they will love you as much as I do."

Earl did not return for a week. When he came through the door, Zelda was cross. Her mother's love potion should have kept him close to her and yet, his children drew him from her for more than one day. Zelda believed her beauty should have kept any man by her.

"Did you forget about me?" she barked. "You left me in this home alone."

The home was large and she spent her days burning through the credit cards he gave her. Buying fine gowns and letting the world know she was the new lady of the house. Still, people didn't believe he loved her. Where was Earl Swanson, the man who doted on his wife? She must just be a place filler for the woman he loved. The talk was impossible to ignore.

"My children and I were enjoying the wilderness. I lose time when I'm with them. They are my heart and soul."

"I am your wife. I am your heart and soul now," she cried.

He pulled her into his arms and kissed her deeply. When he finally broke the kiss, he spoke, "Dearest, my children mean the world to me. Without them, I am nothing."

No matter the embrace, or his reasoning, Zelda could not be calmed. "Why did you marry me then?

Will I have to deliver a dozen children to your arms before you love me?"

"No, that is not what I want."

"Then bring them here. To this home. You have dozens of rooms they could easily fill." She could deal with a few brats if she hired the appropriate amount of nannies and staff. Lord knows, the handful of maids and servants Earl had in the home weren't nearly enough to deal with her demands.

"I would never dishonor my late wife in such a way."

"Yet, you dishonor me. Your wife." Zelda stormed from the home and out into the gardens. Summoning her mother, she demanded her help.

"Daughter, you set your sights on a king among men, they are not the easiest to tame."

"Big men have big egos. I stroked it, I stroked him, why are his children still an issue?"

"Make them a non issue, remove them from the situation."

"He has them hidden away somewhere on this property. Ten thousand acres isn't easy to navigate, especially when he's let it run wild."

"You shall find them, charm them, and send them away."

CHAPTER ONE

"Hello," a sweet woman's voice called.

Elsa's head perked up.

"Children."

Her twin brothers Lars and Liam were working on a puzzle in the middle of the hallway. At one time, the seven Swanson children had a nanny, but ever since her oldest brother Bjorn turned twelve a few years ago, their mother felt they were old enough to care for themselves. Now, they ranged from the eight-year-old twins to sixteen. She wondered if other children were left alone to raise themselves.

When their mother had come to visit them, she told them stories of children being taken away from their families by evil men. That is why she hid them away deep on their father's estate. No one was to know where they were and the nanny had passed away recently. Could this be the woman her father had married? He'd told them about her on his last visit, saying they might come out of hiding. Although, she had only known the sweet love of her parents and brothers she didn't fear the outside world, even with her mother's tales of the dangers lurking in the shadows.

The twelve-year-old stared at her reflection in the mirror. Doubt dripped off her as she brushed her long blonde hair. Ponytail? Headband? Maybe a few barrettes? Did she have time for a braid?

The twins scrambled from the floor and rushed to the window.

"She's pretty," Liam said.

With a hand on each of the boys' shoulders Elsa gazed at the woman with rich red hair pulled back into a tight braid that fell to mid back. She was trim with a slight smile and welcoming features. Would she be like Elsa's real mother and come to her tea parties? Or would she think Elsa was too old for such childish things? Maybe she would curl up with them all and knit by the fire. More importantly, would she read to them all when she came for visits? The books her mother read were much better than the ones their teachers assigned for their online school.

"Do you see father with her?" Elsa asked.

"No, but she must be our new mother," Lars reasoned. "We're much too old for a nanny again."

"Not the way you've been doing your homework," Elsa scolded as she ruffled his hair.

"Hello, my name is Zelda, but you can call me mother if you want to," the woman called again.

The twins scurried out the door joining the thunderous sound of her brothers running down the stairs.

"Come on Elsa," Taghe, her fourteen-year-old brother called as he got to the landing.

"Just a minute," she yelled back and smoothed her dress. Deciding a ribbon would do the trick, she wrapped it around her head and tied the bow tight. Although, the kids all had summer feet, as her mother called it, and they usually ran around barefoot everywhere, Elsa knew she needed to make a good impression. Slipping on a pair of ballet flats, she headed for the stairs.

Her feet barely touched the steps and floated down the curved staircase and out to meet her new stepmother. A strange honking noise filled the yard and as she came to the door, cold swept over her. In the yard, she watched as white feathers flew, fluttering in the air and a white blanket was tossed on her brother Viktor. At first, she laughed to see him covered like a ghost until it molded to his body that shifted and crumpled to the ground. Soon, the squawking came from Viktor and Elsa couldn't believe her eyes.

Her brother had turned into a swan.

Stepping into the sun, sure her eyes were playing tricks on her, a hard breeze blew her back as another swan swooped past her, catching the white blanket as he did. Her new stepmother scowled. Elsa saw the open meadow surrounding her house had six swans stumbling and flying about. A few figured out how to fly and took off after her new mother who swatted them with her bag.

"I'll get you yet," she promised with a long finger pointed directly at Elsa and a harsh chill ran down her back.

With its wings wide in front of her, one of the swans honked and flapped until she got the message. Run. Run fast, run far, and get away before she too, would be trapped as a swan.

Elsa ran behind the house as fear gripped her. Heart pounding hard in her chest her feet slipped on the wet leaves that had fallen recently. Deep reds, oranges, and yellows coated the forest floor. There were no paths in the forest, even though she and her brothers regularly played in it. She knew the trees, at least the ones closest to her home, so at first, she maneuvered through thick roots and uneven ground. Her lungs tightened as she ventured further and no longer could hear the harsh call of her brothers.

Soon, she was surrounded by unknown trees and was unable to catch her breath. In the distance, she heard water flowing. Following the sound, she used the large trees to help keep her upright as she leaned her back against an old oak.

She coughed and cried trying to come to grips with what had to be a prank. Her brothers loved to tease her and found ways to make the others laugh. Only it wasn't a joke. Visions of Viktor's body contorting assaulted her mind. His neck stretching as he cried for help only to have a blaring noise escape. No, she reasoned. They would come find her and take her back to the house. Hans, the second oldest, was addicted to books about magic and tricking the mind. That had to be the case.

Crawling underneath a broad pine tree, she closed her eyes and curled into a ball on the forest floor. The sun would be setting soon and she realized she had to have been gone for hours now. Her lids were too heavy to try to fight against the impending darkness and all she wanted was for her brothers to tell her it was all a dream. The sooner she slept, the sooner she'd wake and this nightmare would be over.

The morning light fought with Elsa's rumbling belly to see who would get her up first. Her shoes were covered in muck and at some point yesterday, a stick had poked through the bottom. Deciding to use her summer feet, she kicked off her shoes and went in search of the source of the sound of water. A small ravine was easier to navigate than the forest floor and she saw huckleberry bushes on the other side of the slowly flowing creek.

Gathering the bottom of her dress in her hands, cold bit at her toes as she dipped them in the water. The iced creek flowed down from a mountain she saw in the distance. Curling her toes around the smoothed stones in the shallow water, she chose to walk cautiously because a cold wet dress would surely kill her. Even now, her body trembled and her teeth chattered trying to warm her up. She wished for the sweater she'd made with her mother last year. The soft chenille yarn they had used kept her warm all winter and even though she'd grown right now, it could be her savior.

Her feet sank into the soft sand of the creek bed and once again, she was torn between the insulation of the sand or walking the ten feet to the huckleberries. With a rumble in her belly, the decision was made.

"At least, I can eat," she said and picked at the berries. The bluish-purple berry burst with flavor as she picked one whole bush clean, staining her fingers and lips deep indigo. "What would Bjorn do right now?"

"I've been to mother and father's home before," Bjorn told the younger children as they sat eating cereal one morning. *"It is grand and beautiful. They even have a little pond if you follow a stone path mother put in."*

A pond had to come from somewhere, Elsa reasoned and picked as many berries as she could hold before setting off along the creek. The sun moved across the sky. Sand that covered her feet had all sloughed off. At least, there was soft grass along the way. When the sky began to turn pink and purple she knew, she would have to find another place to sleep.

Under the pine tree the night before, she'd found a soft bed of needles and the branches were like a blanket. Maybe once again, she could be tucked in away from the world. How far had she traveled? She stayed with the creek allowing her to get a cool drink when needed and a variety of berries bushes still had their fruit. She'd found fallen nuts and added them to her stash after she ripped the bottom of her dress to create a pouch. The extra cool water on her ankles was nothing compared to knowing she had food when she found herself in another barren area.

For five days, she wandered through the forest. Mud covered feet weren't worth dipping in the water as she walked along the shore. Until she had found her father's home, she would save time by not bathing. At this point, she couldn't even go back to the home she shared with her brothers. Her wandering had her lost in a way she had never known.

The creek twisted and turned. Around each bend, she found a new source of food. Nothing substantial, but enough to keep her going. If it weren't for having to walk each day, she could grow fat on the land her father owned. She wondered if he owned the whole world or they were the only family. How had he found this woman Zelda when it seemed as if no one else existed in the world?

The sun began to set on the fifth day when a miracle happened. A loud honking noise came from the sky and she turned her head to see six swans flying in a V.

"Bjorn, Hans, Taghe, Viktor, Lars, Liam," she screamed out in roll call style. She was cold and ached. "Swanson boys!"

The swans cut and moved to circle around.

She waved her hands and shrieked their names again. Over and over until her voice was hoarse.

They circled, then returned to the direction they were going.

She ran as fast as her fatigued legs could muster. This time, she didn't stop, not even when something stabbed the sole of her foot or if she fell. She scrambled back up and ignored the blood dripping down her knee. The bits of dirt and pebbles stung her skin, but still she did not give up. These birds were leading her somewhere. Anywhere, but no matter the destination, hope filled her chest and she knew in her heart she would find her brothers soon.

Bursting between a set of bushes, she watched the swans circle and come to rest on a placid lake. Slowing, she stood at the shore.

One of the swan's head dipped in the water and suddenly came up with a fish between its beak. It tossed it toward the shoreline and soon the others followed suit. Fish flapped at her feet gasping their final breaths.

Tears muddied her vision because in her heart, she knew she had found her brothers. Hope filled her until the final fish was flipped and smacked her in the face. The six swans let out whoops as their wings flapped against the lake as if they were clapping in approval.

"Hans, is that you?" she called as a bevy of swans skimmed across the lake and walked up on the grass that surrounded the lake. "Brothers?" she questioned as they circled her.

When the light started to fade, the swans led her to a cave by the pond. Once inside, she saw a pile of clothes as the boys began squawking and honking. Unlike the playful sounds outside these were pained and she watched their bodies once again become human. They gathered their clothes and dressed. Once Bjorn had his pants on, she ran to them and held tight. Her oldest brother was over a foot taller than her. His arms thick and protective. Soon, she was encircled by warmth she hadn't felt for days. Her body that had shivered against the cool nights and harsh winds, finally thawed.

"Lars, Viktor it's your night to make the fire," Bjorn ordered.

"A fire," Elsa sighed in relief.

"We're not eating those fish raw," Hans called and the back of his hand slapped Taghe's chest to help him gather their catch. "At least not, when we have options."

"What is going on?" Elsa asked as she let Bjorn finish dressing. "Are you free now?"

"Not really," he replied as he helped her younger brothers with the fire. "Every night, we change back until the sun rises. We gathered clothes and found this cave."

"So we can still be together," she gushed.

"We'll have to migrate. We can already feel the urge coming over us to go further south. Once the ice forms on the lake, we will be gone. Spring and fall we can be here for a little bit we guess."

"Elsa…" Liam brought a blanket to her and wrapped it around her shoulders. "We have a few extra things we've gathered. We'll get you clothes tomorrow too. Will you stay here?"

"Of course. I was trying to find the way back to father's. I wanted to warn him about Zelda, tell him what she did."

"Over the next few weeks, we will find a path that will be easy for you. It's simpler with a bird's eye view."

She spent two glorious weeks with her brothers staying up late into the night and getting up early enough that they didn't rip their clothes in the transition. Elsa did her own gathering of food to go along with the fish the boys caught. On their last night, she noticed the boys were twitching from the need to move on.

"I will make Zelda turn you back. No matter what it takes, I will make father believe."

"She can't," Viktor said.

Hans shot him a nasty glare.

"What do you mean? She changed you, she can turn you back."

"It's not the way it works," Hans said as he flopped his long blond bangs back and his cornflower blue eyes were solemn. "We found a way, but we have to do it ourselves."

"What's is it? Can I help?" Hope swelled in her heart as she clasped her hands in front of her chest. "Please tell me."

"We found Zelda's witch of a mother," Hans continued. "She helped Zelda create the curse. After a few choice words—" All of her brothers refused to make eye contact with her and she wondered if her strong brothers may have done more than spoken with the witch. Lord knows violence had peppered her mind. Hans shook his head and continued. "We need to commit to not communicate or make noise for six years as we spin nettles into yarn and make us each a sweater. Although, we think we can do it, basically we're trying to see who can be the quietest. Only one needs to do it."

"Then let me. I'm out here anyway. If father can't help, I might as well stay here. I have food, water, shelter. You've taught me to build a fire. I can save you." She took Hans' face in her hands. "You saved me from becoming a swan with your quick thinking."

"There's a difference between grabbing a sheet and spending six years not able to speak, cry out in pain or even write a letter. You would be picking nettles that are painful and stamping them down with your feet to get the string in them. Six years of knitting while trying to survive. Worst yet, if you screw up and say hi to someone, you can't just start over. We'll die. It's a final solution once you pick your first nettle. Elsa, what about when we come back? You'll want to talk to us. We can't even go off on our own it's why we're trying to figure out a way on our own."

"Trust me," she cried.

"No, we'll find another way."

"Dearest sister, we shall be fine. Stay here," Bjorn said. "We have created a place for you and you'll be safe. There is no way anyone could find you here. Don't go to father. He might be under a spell of that witch same as we are. This winter, we will discover a way to all be together again."

"Promise me, you'll be back in the spring," she cried getting her last set of hugs. "Promise me."

They did before their bodies shifted and feathers floated to the ground and she gathered a handful of them. Tears filled her eyes knowing this would be the last time she saw them flying over the frozen lake and she held her arms tight to her body. She would save them. One way or another, this would not be the last time she saw them. Scribbling a note, she pledged to herself and them that the next time, she would have six sweaters and their family would become whole again. She would be a woman then, six years without the brothers she saw daily would be painful, but she no longer had the protection of childhood to keep her back from doing what needed to be done. Elsa must grow-up, or her family would be lost forever.

CHAPTER TWO

Six Years Later...

Duke King understood many things, but never in his life would he understand his father's need for buying land only to not use it. There were national parks and nature preserves a plenty. Why did his father want to have his own? More importantly, why did he think the wilderness needed to be gardened? Wasn't the point to let the land be as nature intended?

"We will extend the gate to include it in our property," his father Tredmont stated as he laid the map out in front of the Duke.

The dark skin Duke inherited shimmered off his father's shaved head. Standing six-three, his dad made his own way in the world to become a giant in the medical field. Having created a valve that had saved millions and made his father's medical practice secondary to his patent earnings. There was a long shadow from his father and Duke lived in it. To the point, he was currently earning his M.D. focusing in surgery and was poised to take his practice as if the man would ever retire. Not that the twenty-six-year-old was ready for unassisted surgery, let alone taking over a practice.

"Tell me son, have you ever seen more beautiful land?"

"No, it is gorgeous."

"I'm hoping to not destroy too much when I build."

"The fence?"

"The homes. I want luxury homes tucked away, but the fence will make it a gated community. Each home would be surrounded by trees and trails."

"Seriously? Since when are you a real estate tycoon?"

"It's called diversifying. Health care is changing. The malpractice insurance. Shit, the medical insurance is all about write offs. Doesn't matter that I'm saving a life and the people pay their premiums every month. Nope, it's not about healthcare, it's about who can do it for the least amount of money." His father's lips firmed into a frown. "I want to give you an inheritance. A kingdom, that is yours for all to see and will keep you solvent."

"If you're selling the houses, how does that work?"

"We'll own the land. Be in charge of the homeowners association and if we do this right, we wouldn't sell the last house for decades. We have thousands of acres that have been untouched for generations. The woman selling it to me, Zelda

Swanson, said her late husband had left it to his children, but they haven't been seen in almost six years. In a month, she inherits and we can close the deal."

"This isn't our land yet?" Duke asked.

"She said we could start clearing away the land whenever we want."

"I wouldn't drop a dime on property we don't own."

"Clear some weeds maybe." His father kicked at a few rocks as they hiked along a path and came upon a cave. "The little surveying the land has had, showed there were caves and openings all over the property."

"You up for a little spelunking?" Duke challenged his dad. "Or you too old?"

"I'll show you old," his dad said as he made his way to the opening of the cave.

Darkness enveloped them once they made it five feet in and the cave turned sharply to the right, so the sun from outside could no longer light their way. A chill ran up Duke's spine as he took out his phone and turned on the flashlight app. Long stalactite hung from the ceiling coming to a sharp point with a steady drip of water falling into a small pool. Once again, the cave cut a harsh left curve, this time to the left and a light drew the two men.

A small fire burned.

"We have a squatter," his father said as he kicked at a sleeping bag and some blankets.

"You didn't see anyone hanging around did you?" Duke asked.

They were at a dead end in the cave and the small room had a few pieces of clothing, a handful of dishes and knitting supplies. He picked up one of the brown balls of yarn. It was rougher than wool and couldn't be comfortable in any way.

The sound of soft footsteps made them both turn to see a woman with long blonde hair. Her face was one of shock, but she didn't scream. Instead, her eyes became saucers, but she wasn't focused on him. She was staring at the yarn in his hand.

"I'm sorry," he said putting the yarn back in the basket and noticed his hand began to itch. "We didn't know anyone was living here."

"Are you okay?" his father asked. "It's not healthy to have a fire going with no real ventilation."

The young woman backed up until she was against the wall.

Duke wondered how long she'd lived here. She was barefoot, but he saw some small well-worn boots in the corner. Her dress was too short for her, but she had a long cloak around her neck. In her hand was a woven basket with a variety of fruits and vegetables. Water dripped from a fish hanging on a string.

His father tapped Duke's chest and they kept a wide birth as they walked around her.

She instantly moved to the corner with the yarn. She was just a wisp of a woman, but when she moved, the gown pulled tight to her body.

They only got around the corner when his father stopped. "We need to get her out of here," he said.

"She isn't asking for help." Duke itched his palm, the irritation increased with heat that snaked its way up his forearm. He didn't know what the yarn was made of, but it triggered allergens along his skin.

"Does this look sanitary? You're scratching like a wild man from some infectious nastiness in there. Lord knows, what she's got growing on her. She's covered in dirt and wild." His father's eyebrows knitted together. "The carbon monoxide levels alone could have caused her brain damage. It's a health issue."

"Or you don't want a vagrant on your property. Don't pretend you care about her welfare. You want to bring her into town and drop her at a shelter."

Crossing his arms, his father's face twisted to the side. "What would you suggest?"

"Let's take her in and give her a work up. Find out if she has a family." Duke's stomach clenched knowing his next comment was going to get him the side eye. "We could let her stay at our house. For all you know, she might have some squatter's rights. I don't see people dropping a few million to live in a place with some weird *Nell* girl crying about *skewer in da belly*."

Turning his head to the final chamber of the cave, his father nodded. "What if we need to drag her out of here kicking and screaming?"

"Let me talk to her." Duke tended to do well connecting with patients when he did his rounds at the hospital. "She might have some mental issues that have gone untreated."

"Residency rears its ugly head. I suppose I should be happy you're still at the stage where you care about the patient. Fine, but if you can't get her out of here, I'm letting Zelda know and we'll get the cops involved."

Elsa dumped her food into a pot and bundled her brother's sweaters into her basket. She was on the last one and for six years, she hadn't been bothered one day by another human being. Her only friends were the few small animals who didn't see her as a predator. They were short interactions with very few return visits, but it was nice to have another living being to touch.

Although, she had the map her brother's drew, she'd never ventured toward town. The only items she had were the ones she took from the cave by the pond where her brothers spent the spring and fall. She'd watched them from afar each year, but didn't let her presence be known. The hardest was the first year when Liam ran out with is blond curls bouncing as he read the letter to her brothers. Tears streamed down his face and every molecule in her body wanted to pull him in her arms and tell him it would be okay. That was the problem. She wanted to be with them. To laugh and tell stories of her adventures as they told her about the world they now had full access to.

"Hello," the younger of the two men came around the corner.

Immediately, Elsa locked her arms around her belly, so the two baskets were safe on her arms.

"My name is Duke, my father and I were exploring."

His eyes were kind in the dull light of her home. She always kept thee fire low because she didn't dare let it get much bigger when she was not there to attend it. Sometimes, she lit one in the first curve of the cave, so it could be bigger and the smoke got sucked out the front. He was taller than she, at least a half a foot with skin darker than she had ever seen in real life. In books, yes, but her limited exposure to the world rarely gave her insight to a different color hair or eyes, let alone skin tone.

When she noticed his hand, an ache she knew all too well mimicked itself on her skin. For the most part, she could push past the reaction she had to the nettles. Much like being stung a thousand times and no longer even noticing until the rash started. She set down the baskets and found one of the jewelweed stems she'd plucked. One of God's little ways of balancing the world. Where poisonous plants grow, so do their cure.

With a quick snap, she gathered a few cooling drops from the stem and curled her fingers in a beckoning call.

The man extended his palms to her and she massaged it into his skin. His palms were soft and clean. Working her way up his muscular forearms made it so she had to snap the stem a few more times.

"Wow, thank you," he said. "That was driving me crazy. You know there are better yarns you could use."

She gave him a meek smile and gathered her baskets tight to her again.

"My dad was right about the fire. It could be doing damage to your lungs or brain. Would you be willing to come with us into the hospital, so we could run tests? I'm a doctor, well almost a doctor and my dad is a leading physician in his field."

She shifted and the hard wall gave her a base to prop herself up against. Duke's voice was smooth and calming. Tingles trickled through her body she'd never experienced before. The urge to talk and beg for help ate at her. She'd picked all the nettles in her area to the point the invasive weed was almost non-existent. Now she had to travel for three to four days to gather as much as she could carry and bring them back here. She had been preparing to go, knowing the deadline for the sweaters was fast approaching.

"If the hospital scares you, we could go to our home," Duke said.

Home. A real bed. A blanket that hadn't been washed in the creek when the smell got too much for her. The chance at a warm shower, instead of the cold waters coming down from the mountain. All of these dreams she'd put aside for when her brothers returned. When she'd completed her task. Now a man with broad shoulders and thick arms was offering luxuries both on a silver platter. Only how would she find her brothers when she was done with her sweaters? She couldn't speak to ask to come back and although, she knew the forest now, she didn't know the town.

She shook her head and squatted down on the floor.

"Okay," he acquiesced. "How about we go out in the fresh air? We don't have to go any farther than the opening of this cave."

With her baskets still tight on her arms she stood, but didn't step forward until he walked out of her home. Strange, how her life had turned so much and what would have once been a bad dream had become her everyday normal. This was who and what she was now. The silent strange girl who lived alone in a cave with only her memories of good times to keep her from losing the little bit of her mind she had left. Even now, she questioned if this man was real.

Following the curve into the darkness, she knew every step to take to avoid rocks and water. The water from the ceiling was metallic in flavor and she only used it to wash her feet once inside. Mostly, she avoided it even though the rhythmic drip hitting the small pool helped her keep time when knitting and rocked her to sleep at night.

The older man with a shaved head stood at the mouth of the cave. He had a small device in his hand with a screen glowing bright. His finger poked and swiped across the screen. She wondered if it were a small computer like the ones they used to attend school on. Funny, she never thought she'd miss her online classes with teachers she never saw and chat rooms with strangers. They had limited access to the internet when she was younger. The parental controls were encrypted in a way even Bjorn couldn't break.

"Fresh air," Duke said. "That's all I ask. This is my father Tredmont. Tredmont and Duke King. We live on the other side of the fence. It wouldn't take long to get there. Even by foot."

"You want to walk a barefooted woman through the forest?" his father mocked.

"She's already walking barefoot through the forest. What's a little bit further?"

"We can't sit here playing games all day. Either she comes with us or we have the police take care of her."

A bristle of fear tore through her. Her face blanched and for the first time in years, she had to fight to hold in her cry of *no*. They didn't understand the place she was in, she needed only a few more weeks. Just enough time to finish the last sweater. Her head shook as she backed into the cave.

Duke followed with his palms facing down, but out. "Honey, we're not calling the cops."

"The hell I won't," Tredmont barked.

"Dad," Duke scolded and turned his head to the side. "Let me bring her back to our house and get cleaned up. Can't you see she's petrified? The last thing we want is to make her worse."

His eyes turned back to her and she saw they were a deep brown. Almost to the point of black, yet soft. Reminding her of the deer, she had been able to pet when she shared some of the wild strawberries she found in the summertime.

"I told you my name, it's Duke. And my father Tredmont. Can you give me your name?"

His full lips mesmerized her as he requested such a simple thing. *Elsa,* she replied in her mind. *My name is Elsa and I'm not crazy even though telling you my brothers were turned into swans makes me feel that way. But they did. In a few weeks, they'll be back and you can see them. That's why I can't go with you even though every part of me is dying to.*

"I need to call you something. Do you have a name?"

She nodded.

"There's a start."

"Do you write?"

It had been years since she'd read or written anything. Even then, most of what she had done was on a computer. Communication. Had she already cursed her brothers to death by shaking her head? No. They said noise, talking, writing. All of those were forbidden. She wouldn't allow herself to believe anything else.

Shaking her head, she lied to the man who was just trying to help her.

"Okay. Jane Doe seems a bit simple for a woman of beauty and grace such as yourself."

Her heart skipped. Beautiful? She hadn't seen a brush or proper bath in years. Her clothes were tattered and torn. The fabric stretched to the limits by her developing body and yet, Duke called her beautiful. Even in her run down state.

"Is that a sparkle in your eyes? You liked that huh? Well, I'm not going to call a woman girl, and Jane's out. Guess I'm going to have to find a name for you. How about you and I walk to my house and discuss it?"

Elsa had never been to the edge of her father's property. When gathering nettles, she went in the direction of his home. Never the other way.

It took half a day to walk it with Duke. His father drove a large car and went ahead. Duke had an extra pair of shoes and socks in the trunk and she now trotted along with shoes three sizes too big. The cushion of the sole and warmth of the socks made it worth her having to walk a bit awkward.

When they reached the fence, he opened the gate, and she found a well manicured lawn and large home with three stories of bright open windows. The bottom level was all glass with stark gray walls on the second and third story of the square house with sharp lines.

"It looks a bit sterile on the outside," Duke explained. "You'd think my father would want to get away from the hospital. Inside though, it's warm, my mother insisted when she was still alive."

Elsa turned to him and placed a delicate hand on his forearm. As if the touch of a stranger could take away the pain of losing a mother.

He didn't pull back from her gesture. Instead, he placed his hand over hers. "Is your mother alive?"

She shook her head.

"What about your father?"

She turned her head to the side. Having never walked all the way to her father's home she honestly didn't know.

"Do you have any other family? Anyone in the woods?"

The two questions had very different answers. Her brothers were alive, though she didn't know how far north they were at the moment.

"Lets back up. Do you have any other family?"

She nodded.

"Are they in the woods?"

She turned her head to the sky and let the last of the sun's rays warm her face. They were in the air right now. Flying around to her. To where she was and would be giving them their freedom. No longer would the urge to move because it was too warm overtake them. They could be with her.

"Alright. Well, you have family, which is good. But tell me this can you speak?"

She shook her head. It was a lie, but then again, being held against her will is the same thing. It wasn't a question of could she…she just couldn't. Not and keep her brothers safe.

"Are you ready to go inside?" he asked.

Elsa gave him a quick nod.

Duke had never talked so much in one day. The one sided conversation didn't garner much from the waif like beauty, but at least he kept her moving. It was when he gave her the socks from his workout bag that he almost lost his composure.

The tears in her eyes as she pulled them onto her tiny feet. Her dirt covered toes wiggled and she let out a breath of relief when they covered her feet. The shoes were the kicker though. She reminded him of when he used to tromp around the house in his dad's dress shoes. Trying to step without having his foot fall out and the shoe drop to the floor.

Along the way, he noticed her lips had a bluish tint to them. Her fingers had the same coloring only to an almost black. He assessed her with every step. Once he determined she didn't have respiratory issues, he moved to vascular.

Then they passed a bush, she picked the berries and offered them to him.

Normally, he wasn't one to eat anything that didn't come from a reputable market, but she popped a few in her mouth without a thought. The juice could serve as a potent dye. Hopefully, after a shower, she'd lose the hue that on any given day, would have him ordering oxygen by mask.

Standing outside the door to his father's home, he watched as she peered through the windows on the main floor. It must seem strange to have a set of solid steel double doors surrounded by glass. Then again, he wasn't a designer. That was his father's passion.

"You ready?" he asked offering his hand.

Her arms tightened around her waist as the baskets of the harsh yarn had to be digging into her bare arms. Her head turned to look back on the trail they had walked. Her eyes remained fixed on the fence.

He tapped her shoulder, she jumped and inhaled sharply.

"You walked all this way with me. Why don't we see if we have shoes that fit you inside? If not, I'd be happy to take you into town for a whole new wardrobe. Clothes, shoes, maybe a pretty necklace."

She nibbled on her bottom lip, closed her eyes for a minute, then gave him a soft nod.

He once again, held his palm up and her fingers intertwined with his. A spark flew through his body at the light touch and he had to calm himself. This woman had to be of age, but that didn't change the fact she needed caring for. The last thing she needed was a man pawing at her.

His father's home defined open concept. Through the window, she had to have seen the living room and kitchen. All with the latest features, though to her, they may seem completely foreign. They were greeted by a suspended staircase, that may be structurally sound, but even he was nervous when he bounded up them to the second floor. Her hand trembled and he swapped out hands, so he could place a hand on her back as he guided her up the stairs.

"The shower is pretty simple," he explained as he turned on the spray and placed his hand in to ensure it didn't come out freezing. "If it's too hot, you can use this one to turn it down."

She placed her hand palm up in the water and smiled.

He took the cue and dug through the cabinets for his father's hotel procured toiletries. "For your hair, first, then this. Do you prefer a bar or liquid soap for your body?"

She reached for the bar and examined the shampoo and conditioner.

"I—" he stopped himself from offering to wash her hair. Then he scanned the snarled mess and decided he needed to at least try. "Your hair is going to be hard to clean. If you want, after you take a shower, I could wash it in the sink or better yet, the tub." He pointed to the basin then to her hair. "If you don't mind. I'll get you a robe for after your shower, so you'll be covered. I just know when I was younger, I enjoyed someone scratching my head when they washed it."

Her face turned to the shower then back to him. Placing the bottles in his hand, she gave him a smile then dropped her cloak.

He turned around and reached in the linen closet for a washcloth and towel. On an upper shelf, he took down a terry cloth robe to hang on the hook on the back of the door. Behind him, he felt the steam of the shower and knew she must have opened the glassed door of the shower. Keeping his eyes down, he spun to see her thread bare dress on the floor and her bare feet went to tiptoes then back down as the water began to clear the muck. His father's tile had never seen this level of dirt. Duke found it hard to not smile.

"I'll be back in a few to wash your hair." He looked up thankful for the steam covering parts that would push the limit of what he should see with consent only. The blonde hair had natural curls to it and he couldn't help the warmth growing as he saw her let the water wash down her chest. "You remember how to turn it off?"

She nodded and he left her to scrub down. Yeah, that's a thought he needed to push to the side. He picked up her clothes and baskets.

A loud bang of the glass made him turn as she flung the door open and the body he was trying to avoid stood in front of him flush from the heat of the water. Smooth skin, breasts with hardened tips and a golden V with less hair than he would expect from a woman lost in the woods for years. Pulling himself from the curves and hips, he caught her eyes pleading with him as she reached for the baskets.

"I was just going to put these in the bedroom. I'm not taking them. How about this?" He placed them in the corner by the frosted window furthest from the door. Her breathing slowed and he held her clothes up. "Can I wash these?"

Burn really, the thought, but if she was that petrified of him picking up a basket he wasn't throwing that option out there. She gave him a quick nod then realized she was standing before him naked. The door closed quickly as her face blushed bright pink.

"Fuck me," he groaned when he came from the bathroom. He didn't know if it was a prayer he wanted her to fulfill or a need to release his frustration. She didn't talk, but communication was possible. His words were processed. Understanding meant he could help her and damn…did he want to. With a scolding tone, he spoke to his crotch, "Your dumb ass needs to get under control."

"Tell me how that works out for you," a woman said as she stood in the doorway. Her auburn hair was upswept in a French twist with a spiral of hair on either side of her face. "I've found it is usually better to just give in to the temptation then calming the beast."

Duke held the dirty clothes in front of his cock that slowly lowered after this woman invaded the room.

"Someone showering?" she questioned.

"Yes, who are you?"

"Zelda," she said holding her hand out to him. Long fingers ended in a manicure with sharp points. "Swanson. Your father is buying my land. I heard you found a trespasser. I am so sorry for the inconvenience. I'd be more than happy to take her off your hands."

"She's a bit shy right now. I'm getting her to deal with me first. Psychologically, I don't want to spook or scar her."

Zelda sat on the king size bed, crossed her long legs and smoothed out the bedspread. "You have the same bedside manner your father has. We've been having great conversations, but you seem a bit closer to my age."

"Aren't you a widow?"

"You can be a widow at any age. It just proves you loved someone to death."

Duke placed the clothes on the cushioned stool in the corner of the room. No way in hell, would he leave his lost girl alone with this woman.

CHAPTER THREE

There wasn't enough soap on the bar to make Elsa feel clean. Years of washing herself in the creek was nothing compared to heat eating away against her sore muscles as the grit washed down the drain and away from her. If only the last six years could disappear so easily. Sadly, they couldn't. Not until she finished the last sweater. At least, she started to feel fresher and she was sure her father would pay for any outfits Duke purchased for her. If not, her brothers for sure.

Duke didn't seem like he wanted anything from her but her contentment. He wanted her to feel safe and protected.

The water cooled and the soap was long gone. The glass of the door had completely fogged over and she knew her moment of warm caresses was over. It was time for her to get out. When she opened the door, she saw a billowy white towel on the counter. It reminded her of the cottonwoods releasing a soft fiber into the air. She caught a few in the spring, but never enough to spin. Besides, she didn't have time for such frivolity when her hands needed to knit for her brothers.

Now, she felt like a princess as she dried herself, then put the robe around her arms. Even when her cloak was new, she never felt such decadence. A gentle knock on the door led her to turn the knob.

Duke stood there with a cushioned stool in his hand. "Ready for your shampoo boy?" he teased and she covered her lips with her fingertips. "Your lips and eyes laugh, but you don't make a sound. Is there something wrong with your voice?"

She stood steadfast. No longer could she lie to him. Not him. She missed him in the shower. The smell of his cologne had mingled in the air for a moment, once they were inside the cold house. This bathroom wasn't cold though. It had delightful soaps in the shape of birds and a tree with pink leaves being blown off was painted on the wall.

Duke sat down on the edge of the bathtub and he placed a rolled towel on the rim of the tub. Starting the water with one hand, he used his other to gesture that she should sit on the stool. She did and he reached for her feet. Turning her, so her back was to the tub, he placed his hand on her back. "Lean back," he said giving her support as he lowered her.

There was a sprayer attached to the tub and he used it to rewet her hair. Then he squeezed a bit of liquid in his hand. Soon, his strong fingers were massaging her scalp.

She closed her eyes and couldn't remember a better sensation than Duke's fingers in her hair. Without complaint for the disarray her tresses were in, he rinsed and repeated the shampooing three times. Warmth filled her center and when he placed his hand on the back of her neck to arch it and keep the soap from her eyes…His breath tickled her cheek and her lips parted.

The sky was dark outside the window when they moved into the bedroom. She sat on the edge of the bed as he ran a comb through her hair. Starting at the bottom, he spent half the night detangling her hair.

"I can have a professional take care of your hair," he offered through a yawn. "I'm afraid you might need a bit of a haircut."

If she had been left a sharp enough knife, she would have had one before. Her mother always took such care with her hair. The memory of her brought tears to her eyes.

"We don't have to cut it," he said taking her hands in his.

She shook her head and cupped his cheek leaving one hand in his. His hands were warm and held hers as if he were afraid they would break. The last thing she considered was her breaking. Years of living like the animals foraging enough food to last her through the winter and early spring had taught her a resolve she never imagined when she lived with her brothers. They took care of her, but they taught her as they did. Especially in the final weeks, they were together. Fishing without the use of beaks in the middle of the night, building fires and weaving baskets. Each moment was treasured in her mind as was each word uttered. Memories kept her warm when the wind howled outside her cave and when she wanted to cry out in pain while gathering nettles.

"Shall I make an appointment?"

She nodded.

"Are you hungry? I can't believe that wasn't my first thought."

Holding up her hand, she shook her head again. Although she could always eat, exhaustion was taking over. Her lids drooped and she inched up on the bed toward the pillow. A pillow. What a luxury.

The bed shifted as Duke got up and crossed the room. "My clothes will swim on you, but I wanted to wash your clothes." He passed her a t-shirt and a pair of sweat pants.

She slipped the robe off her shoulder then remembered she wasn't alone and didn't let it drop further. It wouldn't be proper considering she wasn't a child anymore to bare oneself to a stranger.

"I'll leave you to it. You'll be safe here tonight and tomorrow we'll take you to get some proper clothes." Crossing to the door, he showed her how to use the lock. "You don't need to use it, but I hope you know you are safe and we are here to help. Whatever you want, you need only ask."

She looked at the clothes in her hands then back to him. *Stay, stay until I fall asleep. Stay with me.* The sounds of the house were foreign to her when moments of silence left them alone. Reaching out to him, she pulled him to the bed. He took the clue and sat. She held her palm up to him as she walked backward into the bathroom to change.

There was a string on the pants she pulled as tight as she could, then she flipped the waistband three times, but the pants still hung low on her hips. The shirt draped down to her thighs and she wondered if she should just wear that alone. Stepping out of the room, she met his eyes. Nervously, she brushed her hair to the side. When she licked at her lips, his eyes widened.

Scurrying, she crawled into the bed and under the covers. She then pulled them back enough to invite Duke to lay next to her.

"Are you sure?" he asked.

She nodded.

He slipped off his shoes and got in next to her.

His broad chest and thick arms were inviting. When she snuggled in against his body, she couldn't help locking her leg around his and discovering a nook by his shoulder. Soon, she had drifted off to sleep.

Duke moved the spatula around the skillet to keep the scrambled eggs from burning.

His lost girl had clung to him the whole night. When the house made settling noises she'd jump and wake, but never make a sound.

A learned behavior he assumed.

She woke before him and he found her in the corner knitting away on a sweater. When he sat up, she tucked away her work as if he would steal it from her. Taking out a stem of the plant, she used in the cave to sooth his skin she snapped and extracted the liquid to wash her palms, like one would with hand sanitizer.

In the morning light, her hair glowed and his heart quickened when she seemed to float to him. Her hand once again, stroked his cheek and she leaned her forehead on his. Making love to a woman hadn't connected him on such an intimate level as this simple contact. Then again, when was the last time a woman stayed the night in his arms?

Now, his lost girl watched as he spooned the eggs on to a plate and buttered the toast for her. He passed her the fork and she smiled when she took the first bite.

"You don't have to pretend. I'm not the best cook, but you actually woke up before our maid got here."

He retrieved orange juice out of the fridge and poured her a small glass. When she reached for the glass, he observed scars along her arms. There were new scratches and droplets of blood had darkened against her pale skin. He waited until she'd eaten her full before examining her arm.

"Let me help you," he said when she tried to pull her arm away. Her fingers had hard calluses, blisters and a slight rash. "Is this from your knitting?"

Her eyes turned down and he lifted her chin until he could see them again. Was her knitting OCD or some other compulsive disorder? Was it a penance of some sort? Either way, she needed treatment for the injury.

"I can help you with this?"

She shook her head and turned to leave.

"You don't have to go to the hospital. I can treat this here."

Her hand wrapped around the waistband of the sweats she wore and her bare feet tripped their way to the stairs. He followed behind her as she disappeared into the en suite. She had placed the basket against the far wall as he did the day before and dug through to the bottom. When she pulled her hand from the basket, the redness had increased and between her fingers was a long green stem with an orange flower on the end. She snapped the stem and a few small drops of clear liquid dripped onto her hand.

Duke marveled at the natural salve reducing the inflammation once again. Taking the natural remedy, he examined it, but he wasn't big on plant taxonomy and couldn't place it. The cut was not better, but whatever she knitted with had a natural toxin attached to it. "This is the same stuff you used on me?" he asked and she nodded her head. "What about the cuts?"

Her head turned to the side as if they were so insignificant she hadn't considered them before.

"Let me show you my medicine," he explained as he took out a first aid kit. First, he cleaned the wounds with hydrogen peroxide. The bubbling on her skin made her eyes dance and lips curve up. Then he placed antibiotic on her cuts before bandaging the wounds. "You up for a shopping trip in town?

"If she's going in town you might want to check her into a bed at the hospital," his father's deep voice echoed through the bathroom.

Instantly, his lost girl stiffened.

"Dad, I've got this. She's not a problem."

"Has she spoken?" he asked. "Do we know our Jane Doe's name?"

"Not Jane," Duke replied with a quick wink to her before turning to face his father. "We're communicating. She's not a threat."

"You're too soft Duke. Fine, she can stay, but you need to watch her and I want a full panel on her. X-rays, everything, so you better find a way to make sure she's okay neurologically."

"The communication barrier is worrying you?"

"Yes," he said peering around Duke's shoulder his eyes scanned the woman. "Either she's silent because she can't speak or because she's dangerous. Not much in between."

When his father left, Duke turned and dropped to a knee to be at eye level with her as she sat on the closed toilet seat.

"What about the hospital scares you?" he asked as he took her hands in his, stroking his thumbs on the tops of her hands. "If I promise to be the one to collect the blood and perform all the tests, will you agree to go?"

Her eyes widened as she bit on her lower lip.

"Blood huh? Have you ever had a blood test? We take a small needle, very small," he assured and flattened her hand to trace along the thick blue vein on the top of her hand. "And I find a vein. Much like this, but maybe higher up by your elbow. A quick prick, less than the feel of your yarn and I take a little bit of blood. We can make sure you're healthy. The X-ray, is a quick picture. You won't feel a thing, but we can make sure your lungs are healthy." He reached out and placed a hand between her breasts.

She didn't flinch. Instead, her tongue licked her top lip and the connection had been made again. Her hand stroked at his cheek as her pupils dilated.

"I'll need to check your heart too. Your yarn is not healthy. The reaction you have can lead to other issues. My dad is worried about the fact you don't speak. I'd love to hear your voice."

She took his face in her hands and leaned her forehead on his again.

He wondered if in her mind, she was speaking and she thought maybe he could hear her. No matter the reason, he wanted to taste her lips and feel her body against his again. How could a wordless conversation say more to him then the hours of mindless drivel he experienced on bad dates? No matter. She trusted him and the last thing he would do is betray that trust.

The urges she had when around Duke seemed unnatural. Her belly tumbled and swirled, but not like when she ate bad mushrooms or ran a fever. No, it was like Christmas when presents filled their home or the first day of snowfall when everything was quiet and white. Her lips tingled and deep inside, she knew Duke had to be the cause. As if he could put out the flame burning inside her in the most wonderful of ways.

Or maybe, it was the most natural thing of all. When her parents had visited together for birthdays and holidays they slept in the same room. She had caught them kissing in a way different from how they kissed her or her brothers.

Snuggled against Duke there was a layer of protection, but there were stirrings inside her. Ones she wanted to explore, but didn't have the time or ability to ask.

"I've always found when I don't want to do something, I give myself a reward afterward," Duke said as he drove along the black path. "But it's up to you. I was thinking we'd hit the hospital first and get the bad stuff out of the way, then go and get your hair done. We'll go shopping and out to eat. Then I thought maybe you'd want to be better dressed for the hospital. So tell me, which would you rather do?"

Elsa's eyes widened and blinked as she stared at him. How would she answer a non yes or no question?

"I have a feeling you know how to talk," he explained. "How about this, you know your right from your left?"

She nodded.

"Good. Thumbs up left if we go to the hospital first, right for shopping." He gave her a coy smile.

"Oh, and just so you know, both are happening so don't think if you choose shopping first, I'll forget about the hospital."

She cut her eyes at him and gave him a thumbs up with her left hand.

"The hospital it is."

Pulling into the parking lot of the hospital, Elsa understood Duke's comparison to his father's home. Square building, lots of windows, and many stories high. The door in the front parted for them as if they were a set of men to open it upon their arrival. A second set of doors did the same thing.

"Good to see you Duke, what rotation are you on today?" a woman at the front desk asked.

"I'm not, I have a few days off, and I'm helping my father out at the house. This is my friend—" he paused and wrapped his arm around her waist. Heat surged through her body as she looked up at him as if to will him to hear her name on the wind. "She's a bit under the weather, so I'm abusing my privileges a bit."

"Gotta have some perks," the woman with ducks covering her shirt said with a wink. "I believe I saw your father headed to surgery earlier."

Elsa grasped his arm and he gave her a comforting gaze.

"He's a surgeon. Nothing to worry about."

She sighed, but didn't release his arm. The tight embrace eased her nerves. Never had she had so many people around her at one time. They moved as if they were all going to a set destination, some quick some slower as they talked on a phone or with another person. All of it strange and new. Even when her brothers were at their rowdiest, the noise wasn't this loud.

An alert went off. Bells and lights flashed as a *'code blue'* was called for the third floor.

Now the movement increased again, and Duke held her tighter. "It means someone's heart has stopped beating and they need people to help."

Should he be going? Can he restart a heart? Lord knows, hers takes off when he is near. She pressed her palm to his chest and smiled at him.

"Right," he said covering her hand with his. "Their heart. Can you feel mine beating?"

She nodded and he leaned his forehead to hers. *"You make mine speed up,"* she thought hoping he could hear her. *"Can you tell me why? Is it more than excitement?"*

He closed his eyes and pulled away from her. An hour later, she had been poked, peed in a cup, and stood completely frozen until a beep went off. All new experiences. Each one, sans the peeing, Duke stood by her side. Why he needed all of that she didn't understand, but he promised to explain how by giving her those few bits of herself, he would be able to learn more about who she was and if more care was needed.

"Duke," a woman's voice called as they were exiting the hospital and they both turned.

Elsa gasped and tucked herself behind him.

It was her. Zelda the witch. Although her hair was darker, she hadn't aged a day. The shocked expression she exhibited told Elsa so much. The witch's face shifted as she kept her focus singularly on Elsa. "I thought that was you," she purred and reached her hand out to stroke Duke's chest.

Elsa pulled him back so no contact was made with the vile creature.

"A little possessive isn't she?"

"It's good to see you again, Zelda. Why are you here?"

"I'm checking in a few patients."

"You're a doctor?"

"Psychiatrist. You should let me sit down with… has she given you her name yet? Maybe writing it down?"

"She doesn't write."

"Not a word. Poor dear."

Her mock concern made Elsa's blood boil.

"I wonder if she even understands English?"

"We've been able to communicate a bit," Duke explained.

Elsa's fingers curled tightly around his bicep. The thick muscle did not give as he flexed. A shot of electricity sent a frisson of heat down the center of her body.

"Just enough to know her base needs."

"Has she been uncontrollable at all?"

Elsa's throat became dry. She kept one hand tightly locked on his arm and brought the other to her neck. Hoping he would understand she needed something to drink or *this woman wants to kill me.* Either would be acceptable interpretations.

"No, she's been quite accommodating."

"That could switch at any minute," Zelda warned. "Are you checking her in here? I have privileges. I could easily put her in the psych ward, so she's under lock and key."

Duke turned to her.

Elsa bit on her lips. Would he lock her away? She doesn't have her knitting. Would she be able to get out in time to make her way to the pond? *Please, please Duke, keep me with you.*

"The last thing she needs is to be locked away," Duke said as he cupped her cheek in his hand. "I'm taking her for a girl day, minus the other girl, but spoiling her with pampering. Integrating her into everyday life."

"A med student practicing immersion therapy seems a bit risky, I will help you along with the treatment."

"I don't think that will be necessary."

Zelda walked past the two of them and picked up a piece of paper from the desk. "Let's see if our silent girl can hold her tongue and still be in society." She passed the folded paper to Duke and gave Elsa a small smile. "You can brush her hair and put her in your old clothes I assume, but that is not bringing her into the world."

"I wasn't in a rush to bring her to a ball," Duke said with a sigh.

Elsa looked at the paper. A man and woman were dancing on the page and her fingers traced the fancy couple.

"It's a few weeks before the costume ball. The last thing I'd want is my sale to fall through with your father because this woman is psychologically unstable."

Elsa didn't understand the words being said. Sale? Her land? Where was her father? Had he left her? What was psychology? Was it some form of witchcraft?

"Ever since my husband passed away that land has been sitting fallow. Who knows what other creatures may lurk there."

Zelda's eyes seemed to swirl or maybe it was the room. Had she said her husband passed? Elsa's father was dead? She'd been so focused on her own survival she never checked in on her father. Her brothers had been her main priority. Getting them back to normal, so they could explain to their father what had happened. What crazy world they had been thrown into? One where witches cast spells and her mother had been right. The world was dark and scary and people locked up others for being silent?

Duke swallowed hard and guided Elsa away from her stepmother.

Too much was happening at the same time. She wasn't sure if she could take one more thing. A sharp pain made Elsa clench her teeth to avoid crying out. Zelda had yanked out a chunk of her hair. Tears pooled in her eyes from the pain of the attack and she dropped to her knees. The way she'd learned to hold in her howls over the years.

"What the hell?" Duke spat as he glared at Zelda and knelt beside Elsa.

"I saw a bug," Zelda replied innocently. "You might need to shave her head and have her deloused."

"Her hair is clean."

"So you say, but did you have her throat checked? Not even a gurgle of pain. If there isn't a biological reason for her not making a sound then, either she's a sociopath that cannot feel pain or she enjoys it."

Duke rubbed the spot the hair was taken from on Elsa's head. "The tears in her eyes tell me she's not really a tie 'em up and spank me kind of gal."

"My bad, immersion therapy, and all. I've found shoving a person in a pool will get them to swim quicker."

"And never set foot in the water again," Duke growled as he pulled Elsa back up and cradled her in his arms. When he laid a light kiss on the crown of her head all the pain disappeared. Maybe he had healing powers that combated the witch. "We'll get back to you."

Elsa never wanted to see Zelda again. She'd hidden from her for six years. Now, the hard scowl from her stepmother burned against Elsa's soul. If she let her get close, who knew what curse she'd put on her. When Zelda walked away Elsa turned to Duke, took his face in her hands and he wrapped his arms around her. The unnatural urges came over her again and she brought her lips to his. Fire snaked through her body as her spine gave way and she melted against him. The sound of her heart beating echoed in her ears as it pounded against her chest. His lips parted slightly as they went from firm to accepting. Never had her body reacted this way before. Her nipples hardened into tight peeks that burned against the shirt she wore.

Duke's fingers splayed and covered her whole back. Elsa wanted more, whatever that might be. She wanted to feel more of him, have him feel more of her.

A moan worked its way up from the center of her and she broke from the kiss before it escaped.

Once again, she curled into a ball on her knees to hold back the sound before it escaped past her tongue. Her lips burned and if she could control the vocal reaction her body had from his touch she would go for more. Everything. She turned her gaze to Duke.

He stood looking dumbfounded as he stared at her.

CHAPTER FOUR

𝒟uke's lost girl was curled into a ball. Her kiss was animalistic and unsteady, but made his cock harden. Was that why she pulled away? Did she even understand what had happened? He held his hand out and she took it. With a slight tug, he pulled her to his side.

"That was nice," he said a bit unsure if he should encourage her. How could he continue, without feeling as if he were taking advantage of her? But she had been the aggressor. "Have you ever kissed someone before?"

Her face blushed the most delightful shade of pink as her eyes cast down. She nodded slightly.

"You have kissed someone, just not like that?" he determined and got one of her patented nods. "Did you like it?"

Her eyes cut to him, the pink on her cheeks turned into a bright magenta.

Duke suddenly feared her overheating. "I liked it too." She moved toward him and he held his hand out to stop her. "We need to get you to your appointment."

Her face fell a little and he brought his hand to her chin. Tilting it up, he moved until her gaze met his.

Her clear crystal blue eyes were busy with emotions rushing from every direction. Expressive nature in them made the lack of discussion a moot point.

"When those eyes aren't overwhelmed with a dozen other things and are only focused on me, we can talk about what happened. Right now, I can tell Zelda upset you, you're probably a little overwhelmed by all the new adventures today and it's gotta be hard being around a man as handsome as me," he teased.

She brought her hand to cover her lips and he took it away. He wanted to see the sweet smile that lit up her whole face. In one day, he'd found himself falling in love with her gentle touch and saw forever staring back at him.

They left the hospital and spent the day pampering her. He was surprised when she chose to cut her hair slightly below her jaw line. The thick tresses dropped to the floor and her whole body calmed. As if the weight had held her back. When he explained the nails, she patted him away as if the extravagance was too much. Nothing was too much for her and finally she acquiesced.

The woman examined her rough hands and decided to soak them to try to help with the healing process.

The self-inflicted pain of working with the yarn she used brought him back to Zelda Swanson. Maybe she did enjoy the pain. He'd only touched the stuff for a moment and the itching almost drove him insane.

When they arrived at the mall, he finally saw her acting like a girl. She marveled at the clothes and she tried on a dozen new outfits. Mostly dresses, but he'd been able to talk her into a set of jeans that hugged her in a way he wanted to. How a woman as emaciated as she appeared to him yesterday had curves and hips he couldn't explain. Although he had been digging the baggy set of sweatpants he'd outgrown in high school hanging low on her hips.

She poked her head out of the dressing room one time and beckoned him to come.

Pushing up for the chair where he'd been watching her as she came out and spun in the three-sided mirror he wondered what the issue could be. Looking around he saw the coast was clear before slipping into the tiny dressing room. His lost girl stood bare naked in front of him with the bra straps wrapped around her fingers.

"Okay, first can I talk you into trying on these?" he asked as he held a pair of lace panties out for her to step into.

She did and he slid them up her thighs. They fit snuggly and his hands lingered a bit long on her hips. Stepping in the room had stiffened his cock. Now, with a firm grip on the globes of her ass he leaned down and captured her lips. His left hand moved up her smooth back as they fell against the wall while his right hand slid down her leg and lifted it to lock around his waist. Her fingers, now long with the fake nails dug into his hair and he let out a moan of satisfaction. He wanted her to claw at his back as he buried himself deep inside her. The thought of not only being her first, but making her his and his alone lit a flame inside his chest he couldn't douse.

"I want you so bad," he growled into her ear as he nibbled along her neck. "Do you know what you do to me?"

He prayed she would speak or cry out. Then again, they were in a dressing room with just a curtain separating them from the shoppers. Fuck, that turned him on even more. Lowering her to the small bench in the dressing room, he knelt in front of her and spread her legs.

The pads of his fingers trailed down the center of her body and he watched as her eyes fluttered from the almost non-existent touch. Arriving at the top of the panties he'd just put her in, he cursed his choice. He could have had her naked right now, but the slip of white lace was a nice enticement.

"Do you know what it means to be touched by a man?" he asked in a hushed whisper as his fingers slid down to the crest between her thighs. "To have him enter you and become one with him?"

She shook her head.

"Does it feel good when I touch you?" he asked rubbing the outside of the panties.

Leaning in, he kissed her belly and felt it flutter. This time, her fingers curled around his neck. He kissed a trail over to her hip and when he turned his eyes to hers, she licked at her lip and her hips arched toward him. Inching the lace down her thighs he kept his eyes trained on her for any look that would tell him to stop. Instead, her lids became hooded with desire as the fabric moved down enough to expose her sex. With one last glance, he took in her body and ducked under the panties.

The first kiss to her sex made her gasp, but not in fear. His tongue extended and licked along the crease giving a flick to her clit. She didn't make a sound, but her breathing deepened. Taking her fully into his mouth, Duke claimed her as his. Although, he wanted to do so much more, pleasuring her had him savoring the taste and feel of her body against his. The smell of the soap she'd used to wash still lingered on her, mixing with the sweet taste of her arousal.

Needing to devour her, he lifted her leg to his shoulder exposing her more to him. His tongue swirled and entered her. Any moans of pleasure came from him as her nails dug deep into his neck as she held him to her core. He didn't need her insistence to stay where he was. The sweet taste and knowledge he brought satisfaction to her was enough incentive to lap and suck.

Going slow, he eased his finger inside to find her tight against one digit. His cock had its own heartbeat wanting to be surrounded by the soft folds that were already milking his finger. Her center rippled around him and he thought he might come from a transference of sensations.

"Fuck me," he groaned and bit too loud and he paused for a moment only to have her pull him tight to her again.

Pressed against her, he had to remove his finger and lock his arms around her thighs. Buried inside her, he no longer cared where they were or who he was. He gave himself to a woman who may not even understand the concept, but he would explain it all to her in the end. Explain how she had dug her way inside him to a place he'd lost and yet, she found it in just one day.

When her body convulsed and her flavor switched from sweet to salty, he paused. Giving one last flick of his tongue to her clit, she hissed and released his neck. As he sat back, he took in the glow she exuded with her nipples pebbled and body flushed. Her breathing was uneven and halting.

"Wow," he breathed.

She nodded in agreement.

There was a knock outside the curtain and a woman's voice drifted in, "Is everything all right in there?" she asked.

"Yes," he replied with a wink. "She was having issues clasping her bra. We'll be right out."

"Take your time." He could tell by the woman's tone she didn't mean a word of that.

Yeah, he would be buying every stitch of clothing in this place. Taking off the tag for the panties, he shimmied them up his woman's legs. Then he helped her stand.

She placed a hand on either side of his head and brought it down, so they could touch foreheads for a moment.

"We need to get you dressed and get home. It's getting late," he explained as he tried to shift himself enough to make it less obvious he was hard as a damn rock. "Let me show you how this works. Can you turn around please?" He slid the bra over her arms and clasped it. Brushing her hair aside, he couldn't help taking a few quick nips to her neck.

Gooseflesh erupted along her shoulders and arms.

"What do you want to wear out of here?" he asked brushing his lips along the column of her neck and taking off the tag for the bra. "Do you want all these clothes?"

She shook her head and picked at the clothes as if she were trying to decide which ones to choose.

He grabbed a pair of jeans and a sweater. Taking the tags off of each of them to give to the clerk along with the other clothes. "I'm buying you everything. It's not that much." He didn't know the price, but there were only a dozen or so items.

Opening the curtain, he found the clerk standing there with her arms crossed.

"We'll take these," he said passing her the clothes and then the tags. "She'll be wearing these out of the store."

With a quick nod the clerk went from bitch to 'I'm getting commission' in about two seconds.

His lost girl stayed cuddled up against him and the clerk stuffed the clothes she'd been wearing into the bag. Their last stop was to get her a pair of shoes that weren't three sizes too big.

Once back in his car, he turned to her. "What is your name?" he asked.

She smiled, brought her hand to his face, and stared. He swore she said *yours*, but he knew better. There was no noise, no peep, no mouthed words…still silent. It had to be his mind playing tricks on him that she was his and he was hers.

"I have to go to the hospital for my rotation. It's like school. You understand right?" Duke questioned the next morning after they returned from breakfast.

Elsa nodded, but her school was done on the computer at home. Although, she might have to go outside and gather items for her science class once in a while, she never went to school.

"Our maid is here if you need anything. You remember Helen right?"

Again, she nodded. They met briefly after dinner the night before and she had made them muffins this morning.

Elsa followed Duke around as he got dressed and put his books into a bag. She let out a little sigh and headed into the bathroom to retrieve her knitting. With him gone all day, she could get quite a bit done.

Panic overtook her as she searched for the basket. Her heart pounded as her stomach flipped. Sounds were drowned out as a whistling filled her ears. She was sure she'd left it on the counter. Opening all the cabinets, she dug out the random items that were of no use for her. The basket had the last sweater in it and yarn that had taken her two days to procure.

Duke stood in the doorway, as she became a mad woman searching for the ball of yarn. Towels flew when she went in the linen closet and Duke stepped into the bathroom. Grasping her at the wrists, he turned her to him.

"Hey, what's going on? Calm down."

Using her hands, she tried to make the motion of knitting. He'd picked up on so many of her signals. *Please understand me. It's gone. My knitting is gone.* Her face contorted in pain.

Duke slowly let go of her wrists. "What's wrong?"

She slapped the counter right where the basket had been. The cold of the counter didn't ease the sting that shot up her arm.

"Your basket?" he asked.

She nodded furiously.

"Okay, um, did you move it into the bedroom?"

She took off knowing she hadn't, but still there is always a possibility. Anything is possible. No. The room was spotless. Elsa ran to the cushioned stool where she had hidden the five finished sweaters. Flipping it over, she found them all neatly folded and safe. Still she did not have the one that was over half complete. It was the last one. The one for Liam.

"The bed is made, maybe Helen put the basket away somewhere," Duke suggested.

Elsa took off out of the room. She raced along the stairway and rounded the corner to see Helen loading the dishes into a cabinet. Elsa didn't slow and slammed her toes into the island in the middle of the kitchen as she slapped at the counter to get the woman's attention. Pain shot up her foot and through her ankle. Pushing past the stabbing feeling, she slapped at the counter again.

"Helen," Duke called from behind Elsa and the woman turned. "She had a basket with some knitting in it. Did you move it when you were cleaning?"

"Yes, that woman and your father were talking. She said it was probably filled with fleas or bugs and it should be burned."

Rage tore through Elsa as she turned and collapsed to the ground in defeat. There was no way in the next week; she could get enough nettles to knit a shirt from the start. Stamping them out to extract the string and winding it into a thick enough cord to knit. Tears streamed down her face as a rushing noise filled her ears.

"Is she okay?" Helen asked.

Elsa didn't want to give up, but could it all be for nothing. Every part of her wanted to scream out, but her voice would end her brothers' lives. She'd chosen to make these sweaters and failed. If she spoke now or waited until the time expired which would be worse on her brothers? Should she give him a few more days of hope or tell Duke how she had failed them? Tell him how him taking her from her safe cave, didn't save her life, it ended her brothers. Her chest tightened at all the years she had held out hope, only to have them thrown away. Burnt on a pyre.

"Helen, where did my father take the basket?"

"Out back, he was going to add it to some brush he cleared yesterday while you were in town."

There was a chance!

Once again, she took off like a shot and rounded the house with Duke calling after her. She didn't have time for him, she needed to find Tredmont and stop him. Maybe there was still time. In the back a huge pile of sticks, nettles and other debris were piled high.

"Dad," Duke called. He caught up to her before she ran into the brush right as Zelda walked into view and tossed a match. It erupted in flames, but Elsa could see her basket on the edge running toward it she dove to catch it before the embers could reach it. Rolling in grass, she held it tight to her body.

"Give it to me," Zelda snarled as she scratched and clawed at Elsa to the point she drew blood. "You think I'd let them escape?"

"Hey," Duke shouted as he pulled Zelda from Elsa. "Back off."

"Immersion therapy includes throwing away anchors. She needs to get rid of the bug infested yarn."

"Stop." Duke placed a hand on the ends of the basket, but Elsa had a tight hold to the handle. "I bought you some new yarn. One that won't hurt your skin. How about you let this go and I'll show you the stuff I bought."

Elsa kept her face stern and hard. When Duke reached to stroke her cheek, she pulled away and finally stood. Looking past the gate, she headed back hoping she would find her home before nightfall. It wasn't the distance so much as it was the fact she'd never walked this way.

"Don't," Duke called as he caught her by her upper arms and turned her around. "You can keep the yarn. Hell, tell me how you make it and I'll get you a thousand pounds of the string. I can't let you go back into the wilderness."

She turned to Zelda who stood with her arms crossed next to Duke's father. Even with Duke protecting her, Zelda wouldn't stop her onslaught.

"Hey, it's me and you," he said and she turned to see his deep brown eyes staring into hers. "Me and you. Don't worry about her. If I say you can keep the basket, you can keep the basket. My father won't go against my wishes."

Tears pinpricked her eyes and she pulled her lips in to make a thin line. Duke had not lied to her. He cradled her in his arms when Zelda hurt her and he cared for her scratches. She would lock the door until he came home each night when he went to school. That way, she would be safe. Giving him a tight nod she tried to smile, but her toe throbbed and her skin burned from the punctures.

Duke turned her arm and saw the blood dripping from Zelda's claw marks. "What the hell?" Duke let go of her and stormed toward Zelda. "If you lay one hand on her again, I will end you."

"Duke," his father spat. "You need to calm yourself down. Zelda did nothing but pull that crazy woman from the fire."

"She was in the grass, not the fire."

"She ran toward it. What kind of crazy person does that?"

Crazy, she knew that word well enough. She wasn't crazy, she didn't need to be locked up. Locked away, maybe, but locked up would be bad. She turned her eyes away from the fire. It was too sad to see all those nettles being burned all because she was so close. Would Duke let her pick more?

"You come near her again, and I'll end you." Duke's arm flexed against the button down shirt he wore.

She saw a few spots of blood on the sleeve and covered her arm to try to stem the flow. Never had she had a man bring out so many emotions in her. The dressing room yesterday was an experience like no other. She wanted more, but she was too tired by the time they got home. This morning, she imagined he would show her more about being a woman, but no he had school. Yet, now the familiar fire licked at her veins and pushed aside any other sensation.

"We have a deal in place," his father said. "This deal is for your future. She is not your future. Some dumb, mute girl."

"She may be mute, but she's not dumb and she is my future."

His father let out a roar of laughter. "Now, I don't know who needs the psych ward more. Her or you?"

"Come on," Duke said has he took Elsa's hand and brought her back into the house. He tended her wounds and said she had broken her big toe. It was swelling up, but there was nothing to be done except tape it to the one next to it. "We will have to put you in ballet slippers when we go to the ball."

She quirked her head to the side as she sat on the edge of the bed.

"My father's opinion means quite a bit to me. I want to show him the beautiful woman I see. I want you to go with me to the ball." He passed her the paper and she turned her chin up to smile at him. "I'll take that as a yes. Also, I want to give you something."

He went into the bathroom and came out with a rectangular box. When he opened it, she found thin blue gloves. There seemed to be a million of them in the box.

"These will protect your hands when you knit."

The gloves were thin enough to be like a second skin and were soft on the inside.

"Are you sure you don't want a different yarn? Something softer?"

She shook her head and kissed him in thank you.

"I can get you more," he said with a deep timber to his voice. "Maybe even a case full."

Elsa shook her head. Once she finished Liam's, she would be done and never touch another nettle again. She would be free and she would have a love as great as her mother had.

CHAPTER FIVE

For three days, Duke would bring snacks up to the bedroom and his lost girl would lock herself away until he came home. Explaining the long hours was fine with her. She never complained and when he came, she was there. Usually asleep, with her knitting on her lap.

Today, he was done with his charting early and was home in time to find her an outfit for the ball. He'd searched far and wide, unsure of what she would want. One night, he'd woken up to find her stroking feathers that at one time would have been white. Now they were dingy and yellowed. He watched as she kissed each one and placed them in sweaters she never wore, but spent hours knitting.

"Can you pass me those wings?" he asked the clerk who did.

"They are snow fairy wings."

"They seem pretty generic to me," Duke said to the teenage clerk as he spread them apart and feathers drifted down.

"That's what the package connected to them says." He passed Duke a large plastic zippered bag with make up, stencils and ideas of various gowns sold separately of course.

After checking the return policy, he picked a long flowing dress and drove home. Bounding up the stairs, he found the floor littered with debris and his lost girl nowhere to be found. If ever he needed a name, it was now. He stomped through the weeds that were laid out with thistles catching on the bottom of his scrubs.

"Hello?" he called then went in search of Helen, but she too, was missing.

A cold chill took over his body as he went out the backdoor and called out for Helen. He walked through the gate and started on the trail back to the cave. Maybe Zelda had shown up and threatened her again. She might have run to the only place she felt safe. The autumn leaves were littering the path he had taken with his father when he'd first found her. Urgency took him over and soon, his walk turned into a jog, then an all out run until he heard laughing in the distance.

Cutting through a set of trees, he came out into a clearing with nettles growing rampant through the opening. His lost girl had a dozen butterflies resting on her arms, hair and even one on the end of her nose. That was the laughter, from Helen of course. His girl was quiet and reserved as always. There were bunches of nettles pulled and bundled with twine.

"Hey Duke," Helen called and gave him a slight wave.

His lost girl turned to the side and the butterflies took flight. Swirling around her for a few seconds before finding a wind to take them to the other side of the clearing.

Helen walked over to him as his lost girl began picking again.

"I found her walking back and forth with armfuls of these weeds. I made her throw on an old sweatshirt and gave her gardening gloves. You would have thought I solved world hunger with the hug she gave me." Helen turned a bit with a solemn look on her face. "I don't know what her obsession is with these things, but I can't see your father objecting to free labor. Zelda had mentioned coming over and burning these off the other day. Guess it's a good thing our girl beat her to it. Why don't you head back and grab a long sleeve shirt, so you can help us carry them back?"

"Right. I'll look for some plastic sheeting and she can do whatever she's doing in the garage, instead of on our bed."

"Our bed?" Helen raised an eyebrow at that comment. "I have noticed your bed has been made every morning. You're not taking advantage of this girl? She seems a bit simple."

"She's not. I think she had some trauma and once I get her past it, she'll be showing me things I've never thought about."

"Go get set up and I'll strip down her bed and vacuum up the leavings."

Helen's expression reminded him of when he was younger and she had helped him through the loss of his mother.

"One other thing, she took quite a few of my kitchen utensils to do whatever it is she's doing with these things. They will need to be replaced."

"Like what?"

"My tenderizer and rolling pin. If nothing else, she's keeping me on my toes."

"I'm just happy she feels safe enough to come out of the locked room."

Duke didn't know that nettles had a natural string in them. Now the allergen made sense. How she woven this into thread all those years blew him away. His lost girl seemed to understand when they moved everything to the garage and soon, he was smashing the buds as she used the rolling pin to crack the stems a dozen at a time. Even after spending a day with patients where he should be drinking and talking about care plans with other med students, he felt content to work in silence with her.

Her shorter hair had a natural curl to it and framed her face beautifully. Red marks were beginning to show on her forehead and cheeks from the allergen on her gloves when she wiped at her brow. Still, she did not halt where he had to apply hydrocortisone with in three minutes of an accidental contact. How had she done this in the wilderness without any protection? She should have some sort of tolerance built up in her system, but it only seemed she had an immunity to the pain she was in.

His father came home with Zelda in tow. The attention she showed him had nothing to do with real estate. She wore six-inch heels with a slight strap around her ankle. The tight dress was not what one would wear to a hospital. This was a hundred percent sexually motivated. Strange, since she'd offered herself to him in the same way. The moment Zelda got out of the car and walked toward the garage, his lost girl stood and walked to the edge of the garage. Did she think she would stop her from her craft project? Seemed a bit silly, but the way her face changed he worried about the effect Zelda had on his lost girl.

"Garden project?" his father asked as he surveyed the reason he couldn't get into the stall. "Sweetheart, you have a really bad rash."

"She knows," Duke replied and stepped next to her. "We'll take care of it after this is finished. No reason to keep reapplying cream."

"You think this is normal?" he asked. "This isn't normal."

"She has a plan."

"Oh really?" his father challenged. "Tell me, what's your plan?"

His lost girl's eyes became big as she turned to Duke.

What could he say? Maybe he'd fallen down the insane rabbit hole too.

"Just because there might be an end to this project doesn't mean it's a plan."

"She's working on something," Duke defended.

"We have arts and crafts at the hospital that don't require an elephant size dose of Benadryl to complete," Zelda replied and passed Duke a set of papers. "She's damaging her liver. Her histamine levels are high. You want to tell me another reason why her lipase would be elevated if not for a mastocytosis? She doesn't look like a heavy drinker, then again moonshine could be a secondary factor. This obsession she has with these plants is killing her."

Duke reached for her to come to his arms and she did. She needed a CT or ultrasound and more tests. Who knows how many years she'd spent harvesting the string from inside the nettles. The one plant she used to ease the skin rash wouldn't be enough, especially with how she goes until done and then treats herself. She needs Benadryl, maybe even a shot of it. "I'm going to get you some medicine and we have to clear this away."

She shook her head violently.

They had spent hours on the task. According to Helen, his lost girl had started early that morning.

"It's hurting your body. It could kill you," he said.

Her face turned hard. Her eyes cut to Zelda as if she did anything beside deliver him the labs he'd ordered. Why had they taken so long in the first place? Maybe they'd run them a few times to make sure the levels were correct. Either way, it was there in black and white with an elevated sign screaming to him from the page. What did he know about psychology anyway? A few courses in undergrad hadn't prepared him to think the way he needed to for his girl.

Tears streamed down her cheeks as her whole body shook.

Pain pierced his heart as her eyes pleaded with him. At this point the damage is done. Whatever she was doing couldn't be but a few more days. He held up his hands in surrender. "If I give you medicine will you take it?"

She nodded.

"This is the last time we're doing this, finish what you need finished and it's done."

Her head went up and down again, as her hands came together in prayer.

"She's almost done."

"Are you planning on letting your lung cancer patients keep smoking?" his father challenged. "Or your diabetics, are you dropping them at the donut shop or making them walk there?"

"Making them walk of course. Exercise is good for diabetics."

"Son, you're making me question my investment in your schooling."

"Has she been a problem for you outside of not being able to park in the garage?"

"How about this," his father began. "I'm going to treat you like you're treating her. She's done with her project, you will be too. If there is no reason for her to be here once we get the land sold on the first."

"Fine, between now and then I'm going to prove to you she's not a mute hermit. We'll be going to the ball on Halloween."

"You're taking her to a charity ball?" Zelda cackled.

"It was your idea," he retorted. "The one for the hospital."

"Fine, it will be a great way to end fall and move into winter. The birds are flying south, maybe she should too." Zelda glared at his lost girl.

Who knew a small pill could calm the skin better than jewel weed? Duke even gave her a special soap to wash with and a salve for when she came out of the shower. He was also freshly showered as he came into the bedroom with only a pair of pants slung low on his hips. Elsa smiled when she came out wearing an old t-shirt of his and nothing else.

"How can you stand it?" he asked as he looked at her new balls of yarn in the basket. Tomorrow, she would spend the day working on the sleeves of the sweater. "I still feel like I'm itching all over."

She went back to the bathroom and retrieved the salve he had given her in a tube. Squeezing some into her hand, she offered to apply it to his skin.

"I know I don't have any on my back, but still it feels like I do."

The expanse of his shoulders called to her as she pressed her hand to his back. Massaging the ointment into his thick muscles, she did see a few spots that were irritated, but on his dark skin it was hard to make out any rash. Her fingers trailed down his back and a rush pooled in her belly. His shoulder rolled back and broadened from the touch. Did she dare? She wondered right before her lips touched the center of his back while her fingers circled his waist. When she rested them on the front of his pants, she found a hardness like the one from the day in the dressing room. Her center where he'd kissed tightened and she wondered if her body knew something, she hadn't been taught.

He turned in her arms. Her lips brushed against his nipples and right above his heart.

Tilting her head up, she found him staring at her with hooded eyes. His hands ran under her hair and she rose on her tiptoes to meet his lips.

The world spun and she felt the bed against the back of her knees. It sent a shiver down her body, but not of fear. One of anticipation. He knew what was supposed to happen between them. All she understood was something wonderful would bring them closer to each other. Ever since that moment in the dressing room, she'd wanted more. She needed him to touch her.

Removing her shirt, she stood before him bare.

With a hard swallow, he stepped back.

Meekly, she brought her hand to the center of her chest.

He stood with his hands together. "God, I want to know your name," he said and she turned her eyes down. "Do you understand what you want?"

Her other hand covered her belly. It was spinning and tightening with the idea of him being with her. He'd helped her for hours today. Protected her from Zelda. She wanted to give herself to him. Reaching for his hand, she brought it to her breast. He held it in his hand, his thumb stroked her nipple, and she hissed.

"You like that?" he asked with a light growl as his other hand rested on her hip. "I don't know how to explain sex to you."

Placing her hand over his, she moved it along the side of her body and back down. Wrapping it around to her ass. His fingers curled tight and she smiled up at him.

Taking her other hand, he brought it to the hardness in the front of his pants. "I'm going to show you what I want you to touch. What I want to put inside your body."

Inside? She supposed there were places where objects could enter. His finger entered her and it made her wonder why she hadn't placed her own there. This was larger, harder, and longer. Would it fit? Would it make her shudder? Could she control her voice?

"Not yet," he said as he laid her back on the bed.

Standing at the end, he dropped his pants and she took in the full view of him. The maleness twitched a bit and the urges came back. She wanted to touch it, taste it, taste him. Moving up to her knees, she crawled to the end of the bed and found his lips. Pulling him back with her, he encompassed her body bringing his heat with him.

Her leg curved around his hip and he cupped her thigh. Kissing along the column of her neck her head fell back. His sex rested against her belly and he didn't seem in a hurry to enter her. Instead, his fingers explored her cooled skin. Igniting hot tendrils as they created a trail along her sides. His lips caressed the scorched skin as she arched her back and bit down on her lips.

"Tell me your name," he whispered when he returned to her neck. His teeth nipping the lobe of her ear.

Elsa, she mouthed, but kept her voice silent. *My name is Elsa and I am yours.*

Moving her legs wider, he nestled against her center and began to rock. His hand blocked her entranced as it rubbed circles and electricity crashed against her. One finger, then two widened her. The slickness of her body made the entry smooth and unhalting. He stroked and swirled as he claimed her lips. The circle almost complete with their bodies together.

"Are you sure?" he asked as he broke the embrace. "You want to do this?"

She nodded. Her body was aflame as nerves crashed against her skin in a way she didn't know was possible. How had she not been told this would be coming for her in later life? When she was grown. That a man would come into her life that made her heart sing and her body explode with sinful sensations.

A twinge of pressure caused her to inhale sharply when the tip of him touched her center. Spreading her legs wider allowed him to slowly inch in and she clutched the pillow behind her head. Bracing herself, he eased into her opening, not rushing, but going in and out, each time a little deeper. Stretching her a little wider until with sweat glistening on his brow and he took quick shallow breaths as he balanced on his forearms above her. The tip of him poised at her entrance before he plunged himself fully inside.

Now the circle was complete. His lips on hers as his tongue stroked hers in concert with his hips rocking. He no longer retreated. Instead, he stayed flush against her as she became awash in sensations that made her want to cry out. He did. Moaning and praising her for doing little more than being there. The feel of him whirled through her blood, she felt as if she were floating. Although the bed was beneath her, it was merely a base for him to penetrate her in ways she knew was saved for the one you would marry. Duke had claimed more than her body. From the first moment she met him, she knew he claimed her heart. Deep in a way, that sex had enhanced. Her arms clung to his chest and as his pace quickened, little bursts of pleasures elongated until one continuous wave over took her and she found his mouth. Afraid she'd cry out as her body convulsed and locked on to his hardness. It pulsed against her walls and he collapsed on top of her with a howl.

"Don't move," he said as if she had the ability.

She wondered if they had not truly fused together. She didn't recognize her arms or legs. Every inch of her tingled. His lips brushed her shoulder and she clenched around his softening shaft. Questions bombarded her brain about what had just occurred. It was magical and transformative, but they would have to wait. She had a few days left and many hours of knitting to do before she could speak the words she held tight in her heart.

"Stay with me. Tell me everything. Tell me why you don't speak and why you need to spend half your day with poisonous plants."

He rolled off of her, but pulled her in his arms and reached for the cover to surround them. Wrapped up, tucked away and apart from the world. This could be her happily ever after. He was a king in a way. Much like her father who always said she was a princess. Why couldn't they be just the two of them in a happily ever after scenario? They couldn't. She hadn't destroyed the witch yet. She hadn't saved her brothers. Her indulgence of laying in Duke's arms as their naked bodies intertwined could not go on forever.

Elsa had now, this moment, and she would indulge in one night.

At least Elsa was using the gloves as she knitted when Duke woke in the morning. He pulled her pillow tight to his chest and watched as she moved the sticks she used as needles back and forth. Who was she making these for? An enemy? Helen found a few others hidden in a drawer. There seemed no reason to take them from her. Appearing innocent, she had a need to finish them and he had a feeling stopping her would set back any progress they'd made.

Her body was perfect, as they'd moved together. He'd made love to her four times during the night. Retrieving his phone from the nightstand, he searched his favorite diagnostic site to determine the long term issues his lost girl might face. At least she wasn't turning red from allergens or blistering. She seemed to understand stroking her head, even with the gloves on, would cause the toxin to spread. Limiting the exposure had been key as she sprayed down areas where her basket had been placed. Even now, she might as well be in her small cave the way she crouched tight on the chair.

"Morning," he said and she gave him a small smile. "How are you feeling?"

Her smile widened and she held up her knitting.

Right, he would be second fiddle to that crap until she was done. "I bought you a dress and some wings," he said as he reached for his pants to pull on. "The ball is a costume one. I have to wear a mask basically since I'm a guy. Mask and a tux. I've got it easy."

Retrieving the dress and wings from the closet, he laid them out on the disheveled bed.

She placed her knitting in the basket and took off her gloves. Holding her finger up, she walked into the bathroom and he heard the sink running. She was learning. There was no lacking in cognition. Damn it, one moment he was buried inside her thinking of no place he'd rather be and the next she's back to being a patient. Was it just her? It was. The way she looked at him and touched him—

As if on cue, she walked out in her jeans and sweater and placed a hand on his cheek before gently kissing his lips.

He cupped her cheeks and brought his forehead to hers. A connective gesture she taught him. One he didn't want to break ever.

She walked around him with her hand trailing on his belly.

There was a connection between them at a base level. He wanted her to know it, but how could he express himself in a way she would understand? How long had she been in the wilderness? She took to most things like a long lost friend, but did she understand love? Commitment?

"I love you," he said as he caught her arm before she had moved past him. "I don't know your name, or where you come from. Your family or why you suffer with painful cuts and blisters, but I know I want to spend the rest of my life finding out."

Her face lit up and she nodded her head.

"Do you understand what I mean?"

She brought his left hand to her lips and kissed his ring finger.

Oh, she got it and with that simple caress, he realized he had proposed marriage. This would be a nice grenade to launch at his father. Maybe Christmas morning or something. Or his birthday. What the fuck did he just do? Crystal blue eyes peered up at him and he smiled. He had made the best choice in his life.

"One stipulation," he said. "You will tell me your name before we get married."

There wasn't a moment of hesitation in her eyes. She pointed to the knitting then held his hands together with hers. A small nod brought her forehead to their clasped hands.

"You really can speak can't you?" he asked.

She placed a kiss to his knuckles.

When they broke from the moment, she picked up the fake wings and fluffed the feathers. The gown was long, with white fluff along the skirt. He wasn't sure if she would resemble an angel on a cloud or a swan floating along a pond. Either way, he passed her the mask and she put up her hands to push it away.

"It's just a mask," he replied and tried to place it over his face.

She tore at the fabric that attached a veil on the back.

He didn't understand how it went with the costume outside of the feathers that were attached, but she was not having it. "Okay," he said setting the item aside and holding his hands up. "No masks, but people are going to wonder about me, then if I don't wear one."

Taking off to the bathroom, his lost girl confounded him at times. The mask was a clue though. That he knew. Covering her face had been bad. Good thing he didn't want her to be a ghost. She came out of the bathroom with a handful of makeup that Helen must have dumped there just to get it out of the way. It was zombie makeup from last year.

"You want to be a zombie angel?" he asked.

She shrugged.

"We can do this then. Try on the dress and make sure it fits."

CHAPTER SIX

The night of the ball, Elsa had finally finished the sleeve of the last sweater. In the morning, she would head out to the pond with the cave and save her brothers. She would wait until they arrived. Helen helped her paint her lips and eyes with a full mask. She even placed a halo on her head instead of the veil that reminded her of the sheets that fell and covered her brothers so many years ago.

Each fall, she'd heard the call of her brothers when they flew over the forest to the pond. When she stepped out into the cool crisp air, a set of swans honked as they cut through the sky. She tightened her grip on Duke's arm wanting to follow the birds. They must be her brothers flying over the house toward the pond. Maybe he would be fine with skipping the party. Lord knows, this was more important. They were early. She could have her brothers back and whole by midnight.

"It will be okay. I'll be by your side the whole night," Duke assured her.

Standing still, she watched as the swans disappeared on the horizon.

His hand patted hers and she felt grateful for the care he showed her. For the first time in years, her skin was smooth and soft. Welts and blisters didn't plague her and even with a sore toe, he'd given her comfortable shoes and a pill to ease her pain. What fate had made him wander into her cave? Why had she returned when she did from foraging? Was Zelda lulling her into a false sense of security or had the curse run its course and would she soon be free?

Free to marry a man and have her own children. Be loved and enjoy the touches he lavished her with when she wasn't knitting. He allowed her to complete her task no matter how insane it appeared. When they arrived at the ballroom, women swirled in expensive gowns and jewels. She wasn't the only one with wings, but she was the only one with a halo.

Zelda appeared out of nowhere wearing the garb of her people. The pointed witch's hat was smaller like a doll's placed on her head like Elsa's halo. Her dark hair tumbled down her shoulders to a deep V cut in her dress at her chest. Unlike the witches seen growing up in fairytales, Zelda's dress was tight and hugged her body. It fanned out at the bottom and the sleeves had a ring that slid over her middle fingers. She had an orange mask of cut metal with delicate lines and etching.

"Where's your broom?" Duke asked with a bit of a snarl as his arm wrapped around Elsa's waist.

"Aren't you just the kidder," she cooed in a way that made Elsa's blood boil. "Maybe you both need time in the psych ward. Believing in witches and all."

Elsa squeezed his upper arm and he gave her a nod of acknowledgement. A waiter walked by and Duke reached for a glass of a bubbling drink. She copied the motion and he led her away from Zelda.

"For a therapist, she has no bedside manner," he said as he clinked his glass to hers.

The drink tickled her nose as she took a sip. It was sweet with a hint of a dry after taste. She hadn't had soda since her last birthday. A treat their parents let them enjoy on special occasions. *There is nothing more special than the days you were each born.* Her mother's voice echoed in her mind. Those small memories were becoming less and less as she created new wonderful ones with Duke.

"Do you know how to dance?" he asked.

It had been years, but proper etiquette for parties was a part of her upbringing. Even if her brothers and she never understood the reason. Bjorn did say his studies were changing since his sixteenth birthday. Father had longer discussions about the world and a company he ran. Charity functions like this one, would be something she could have attended once she turned eighteen. In a way, she was fulfilling her parent's dreams for her.

"Follow my lead."

They set their glasses down and he brought his hand under hers to lead her out onto the dance floor. His hand rested on the small of her back, pulling her tight to his body, as the other cupped her hand. She moved backward as he glided around the room. Colorful outfits and classical music filled the air. Maybe because of her injured toe, or perhaps this was the way he danced, her feet only brushed the floor as she floated in his arms. There were many reasons why she hoped for a future and the main one was the man whose arms she was in right now. Could she possibly be his wife? He promised to marry her once she told him her name. It was a good name. A strong one. She had been named for her great grandmother. A woman who had worked side by side with her husband to build an empire that she was now poised to inherit.

There was little Elsa understood of this world, but of one thing she knew. She was a princess in a way. An American princess who was guaranteed certain things in life. Zelda tried to take them from her, but God had a plan and it only made her stronger. She was no longer the sweet little girl who played with dolls well past the age many would have. Elsa helped raise her younger brothers and had responsibilities most would shy away from or feel too privileged to have to take on because of their station in life. Now, she would save them. Once she got home with Duke tonight, she would gather her sweaters and make her way to the pond.

For now, she would create a memory that would get her through the long walk.

Turning her eyes to him, she found him smiling down at her. She wondered what about her, had brought them so close so fast? Is this how it was with love? Did one just know from a slight touch?

His dancing slowed and they were no longer finding their way through the whole floor. Instead, they were rocking in a circle as others danced around them. Duke leaned down and captured her lips while they swayed. Calm washed over her, clearing her mind as the room melted away.

"I love you," he said softly against her lips.

And I you, she thought using every bit of strength in her body to not speak it into the world.

"Your sweaters are done and still you won't tell me your name."

She placed her finger over his lips and raised herself on her tip-toes so she could press her forehead to his. *By this time tomorrow, you will know my name. You will know my brothers and they will tell you of their pain for the last six years. Tomorrow, my love. One more day.*

After three songs, Elsa excused herself to find a restroom. The ballroom was at the top of a grand staircase.

When she walked along the hallway Zelda approached her with a snarl. "You think you can save them? You have less than a day to finish your little arts and crafts project and you use the time to dance and drink. Duke will never love you and by tomorrow at midnight, your brothers will be dead."

Elsa's jaw tightened as she lifted her chin.

Zelda stepped toward her as if she would back down from her.

She was no longer the little twelve-year-old wanting approval from a new mother. This witch had taken everything from Elsa. Her brothers, her father and her home, but that all ended today. When Zelda lifted her hand, Elsa didn't flinch. She'd suffered physical pain without crying out for years, one more day, one more slap or broken bone wouldn't stop her now.

Zelda's palm faced Elsa as she flicked her fingers and an invisible force sent her tumbling back. Her foot slipped on the top step and there was no railing to grab hold to. With arms splayed out, she floated this time without Duke to cradle her back and keep her safe. A sharp pain shot through her spine as she hit the marble stairs only to bounce and flip, turning her face first with no way to slow her momentum down the dozen stairs still in front of her.

Her brother's voice called to her. *We'll die. If you cry out, we will die.*

Injuries piled up along her ribs, spine and hips as she tumbled. Spasms caused her body to contort as she tucked into a ball. People cried out for help as feathers from her wings fluttered around her just like the last time she saw her brothers.

Duke ran down the stairs and slid next to her before the world went black.

"She just slipped on the top step," Zelda explained with pain in her voice. "Not one word or cry came from her as she fell."

"Why do I hear disappointment in your voice as you say that?" Duke snapped as he tried to rouse his lost girl. "Come on baby, I need you to wake up."

Her dress was ripped and the wings destroyed. The angel costume was too iconic at this moment. He couldn't lose his lost girl. Not now, when they were so close. She spoke to him in ways words couldn't convey. People were mumbling around him and when he turned to see Zelda, she had a phone in her hand.

"You better be on the phone with the ambulance," he snarled. "I don't know how you did this, but I know you did."

His silent lost girl was now truly gone to him. Her pulse was strong, but when he lifted her eyelids, the sparkle had left her irises and her pupils barely reacted to the change in light. Concussed and currently unresponsive, Duke's heart tightened to a vice and he feared his own death would surely come on the heels of hers. Kissing her lips, he prayed for a damned miracle as if this were a fairytale and not real life.

She moved under him, but did not make a noise.

"Did she moan?" Zelda asked with a peaked interest.

"No, she didn't," he bemoaned a bit.

Even in her injured state, she maintained the silence he knew now was a vow of some sort. A promise to either herself or another that meant more to her than her own life.

"I'll admit her. She might be suicidal. Once she's cleared medically, she'll need to be moved to a locked ward."

"You have got to be kidding me. Right now? That is what you're worried about."

"Why aren't you?" she challenged as he checked her extremities and pressed her ribs.

She may be battered and bruised, but once she came to, he could deal with that. He could deal with anything as long as she woke up and told him her name.

When they loaded her into the ambulance, she fought against the restraints and he clasped her hand. "I'm a med student, I have privileges can I please ride with her?"

"In the front seat only," the medic said. "You know the rules."

"Son, I'll meet you there," his father called as Duke slid into the passenger seat of the ambulance.

Five hours later, the moonlight shined bright through the darkened room. His lost girl had been scanned from top to bottom. No expense was spared. He had them test her liver and a few other items since she wasn't in a position to argue. Her hand lay lifeless in his. Although she stirred on occasion, her eyes had still not fully opened. On her forehead, a purpling goose egg had an ice pack to try to reduce the swelling.

"Any change?" his father asked as he stood in the doorway.

"Her blood pressure is steady," Duke replied as tears streamed down his cheeks. What he wouldn't give for her controlling him and making him follow what she said with no words.

"I'm not sure what you have against Zelda, but I need you to push past it."

"Why would you bring up her name right now?"

"I asked her to marry me."

Duke sat back at the confession from his father. He wasn't a fool who believed his father would never remarry, but Zelda had a way about her that made him question her motives. It was as if she didn't care which King she landed as long as one of them married her. "Guess the land sale won't be an issue now," Duke stated harshly.

"That's not what this is about."

"There would be no other reason."

"She's beautiful."

"On the surface maybe, but underneath, all I see is a withered old hag trying to get her claws into a man with money." Duke turned his eyes to his father haloed by the light of the hallway. "Why is she so eager to sell the land that has been in the Swanson family for a century?"

"She's a Swanson by name only."

"I've been looking into that family. I remember when they were splashed all over the news when I was a kid. Then they disappeared. A family that built this town, just vanished."

"His wife died and if it weren't for Zelda, he would have killed himself from depression."

"So says Zelda." Duke shook his head. "He had seven children. Seven and not one has come to claim a fortune that was safely locked away in a trust. You know why that is?"

"No clue."

"Zelda's broke. She burned through millions in a handful of years."

"She believes in charity."

"She believes in headlines." Duke scowled. "Do you know how many times I've seen her name associated with charity balls? She hosts, she attends and none of them make sense or seem close to the ice chunk she says is a heart in her chest."

"That woman has more compassion—"

"For social media. For praise and adoration. Two days after her husband died, she flew to the coast to attend a dinner. I think his burial was an after thought."

"Zelda has shown nothing but compassion for your little pet project and I will not have you besmirch her name."

"Pre-nup," Duke said and refocused on his lost girl.

"You're one to talk. How much cash have you thrown on this woman? Her care alone here will be upwards of fifty-thousand dollars. One human life is worth more than another to you."

"It has yet to be proven Zelda's human."

"I'm leaving before you say something you can't take back."

"Love you, dad." Duke made sure his voice was sincere.

"I know you do. This is just a shock to you, I'm sure." He left.

Duke scooted his chair closer to the bed. Dropping his head to the back of her hand, he rested his forehead against the IV providing her fluids. When the sun began to creep across the floor from the sunrise, her hand moved and wiped at the tears on his cheeks. Lifting his head, he saw his lost girl with her eyes droopy, but alive again. The blue pools took in the room as she cupped his cheek.

"You scared me," he confessed as he stood and brought his lips to hers.

She returned the kiss, but as she woke more, she pressed against his chest.

"Are you okay?"

She shook her head and lifted her hand. Pulling at the IV he covered it and tried to calm her down. Removing the nasal cannula from around her head, she spun to the side away from him.

Rushing to the other side of the bed, he steadied her. "Hey lady, you had a big tumble. You need to rest."

She fought him as he pushed her back down in the bed. Her head shook again and she brought her hand to the side. It had to hurt. Shaking wasn't a good idea with a concussion.

"Baby, you have to understand you injured your head and brain. You can't move around, it's going to hurt."

The snaps of her hospital gown sounded in the room and soon she was naked before him with only the hospital issued netted underwear. Purple and blue bruises showed her path down the stairs as they rounded her body and made him physically ill. She pulled at the tube going down her leg.

Duke clamped his hand around it. "This will hurt coming out," he warned. "It's— it's—there's no delicate way to say this, it's inserted in your bladder."

The invasive sensation must have registered and she held her hands up in surrender. Her eyes told a different story. A very different one that let him know she wasn't about to stay in the hospital. Splitting headache or not, his lost girl wanted to go home. Now.

"Can we make a deal?" he asked.

She nodded.

"I'll get all the tubes and wires taken off, if you promise me when we go home you will listen to me. You'll lay in bed and rest."

Something in her eyes made him think she'd abide by his rules until the time suited her and she needed to finish another project. Would he always be chasing her and her crazy ideas? Zelda might be right about her obsessions.

"Your sweaters are done," he offered as a plea to know her name. "I still don't know your name."

She placed her arms in front of her with her right arm straight up in the air. It slowly lowered to her left that was parallel. Pointing outside she flipped her arms and brought her left arm up to create a right angle, then repeated her first action.

"Sunset?" he asked.

She nodded, gathered his hands into hers, and brought them to her forehead.

"At sunset, you'll tell me your name." Duke let out a sigh. "Then I better get you home. It'll be a bit before the doctor will be around. Maybe noon or so, but then we can—"

She shook her head and began peeling off her heart monitors. Alarms sounded and he got up to silence the machines. Stubborn to the point of insanity. Then again, he was going along with her, so who was really the crazy one here? He helped her get unhooked from everything and found her a pair of scrubs. Her chart was at the end of the bed and he signed her out against medical advice. Leaving the paperwork on the bed, they walked out of the hospital and drove home.

"Promise me you'll stay here," he said as he tucked her into the fresh sheets of the king size bed they had been sharing.

She gave him a smile and patted his hand.

"I'm going to go get you food. Are you hungry?"

She nodded and he headed down to make breakfast.

"I was going to say I was surprised to see you here," his father began as he walked into the kitchen. Dressed in jeans and a sweatshirt he knew his father was planning on a day of manual labor outside. "But I had the most interesting phone call from the hospital. It seems a patient I admitted last night left AMA."

"Can't save them all."

"Where is she?" he asked.

"Upstairs and before you start—"

"You're finishing your third year of med school, not residency. Either of which wouldn't make you qualified to say what this woman needs from a medical stand point."

"Not everything can be broke down in *Grey's Anatomy*."

"She has a grade three concussion. The last thing she needs is to be up and moving around."

"That is why she's laying down in bed." Duke smeared the toasted bagel with cream cheese. "I'm bringing her food, drugs and I'll back off her Benadryl until her grogginess has passed."

"She's not a wounded bird you can care for and hope for the best. That woman is—"

"My fiancé," Duke stated shortly. "I asked her a few days ago."

"How? She doesn't talk."

"To me she does. Not verbally, but we talk."

"You talk and she makes hand gestures?"

"If she was deaf that would be a shitty thing to say."

"Is she?"

"No."

"Then drop the politically correct shit." His father began to pace in the kitchen. "What is it about this girl that has you so sprung?"

"We connect. I can't explain it, but to me that means more. When I get up in the morning, it's because I know she will be there sitting in a corner knitting away."

"Duke, you've never been a kid I had to worry about…"

"Then don't start now." Duke knew it didn't make sense, but his lost girl was not crazy and neither was he unless being in love meant you were crazy. Then they both should be locked away.

Bringing the tray up, his stomach clenched when he approached the room. The door stood ajar and he was sure he had closed it. Pushing the door with his foot, he found an empty room. He set the tray on the end of the bed and went into the en suite.

She was gone.

His heart dropped when he went back into the room and saw the drawer with the sweaters was open, but empty.

CHAPTER SEVEN

Elsa pushed past the gate and started down toward her cave. Her old home had all the markers she needed to get back to the pond. The sun was still low enough in the sky, so she knew she had a full day to find her brothers. Her head pounded even with all of the pills she had been given promising relief. Mix that with her foot screaming from the broken toe she knew it would take her longer than usual.

It didn't matter. Only one thing did—her brothers.

When she returned the next day with them by her side, she would call in her own voice for Duke to come to her. She would fall into his arms and tell him her name. They would kiss and she would promise never again, to knit or touch a poisonous plant. They would stay up late and she could tell him all about her family as they planned their own.

When he made love to her, she would call out his name. No longer restrained, her cries could echo through the home as she climaxed. Elsa had grown in his arms and he had helped her discover the strength inside her was greater than even she imagined. By the time she found her way to the cave, she curved her way in the dark to the back where her collected items sat idle.

The fish she had caught rotted and the smell overwhelmed her senses. Surprising because she thought it would have been swiped by a raccoon or some other animal weeks ago. Using her hand, she was able to work her way along the wall until she knelt by the back where the map from her brothers was kept.

Although she trusted her memory, the headache had her mind flashing and she wasn't taking a chance when she was so close to saving her brothers. Coming out of the cave, the light assaulted her injured brain. Holding the paper above her eyes, she made her way to a nearby tree for shade.

While she got her bearings and opened the folded paper, a buck came into view with a deer beside him. He lowered his massive rack of antlers and the doe brought her head to his. The moment lasted, but a few seconds and then was broken as they moved on to a bush she would have picked clean if she still lived out here. They nibbled on the sweet huckleberries that had sustained Elsa for years. Birds chirped as they discussed their flight south or found bits of fur to keep them warm in the winter. Squirrels were in their hyper crazy mode where they fight with each other over a nut that might be their salvation in the coming months.

Never again, would Elsa worry if she had enough fish smoked for winter. Or, if her stores of nuts and mushrooms would sustain her, or if she would have to go in search of food in knee-deep snow.

Nothing changes until you save your brothers. She started out toward the mountains in the west. Every step she took, brought her closer to her brothers. It freed her and them to a life where they could once again play. Pain stabbed at her foot until it throbbed with its own heartbeat, then went numb. Either she blocked out the ache or the foot was dead. Neither option scared her. Determined, she walked with the basket weighing down her arms. Stopping only to scoop up a few handfuls of water from the stream or picking the last of the berries. She didn't want to take too many because banquets would be in her future. Duke making her eggs in the morning and she would learn to make him steak in the evening. Maybe she would return to school and become a doctor like him. The future was open and the concept was enough to quicken her pace.

The sun lowered in the sky when the sound of honking made her break out into a run.

"There she is," someone called, but that was from behind her and the sun was still out, so it couldn't be one of her brothers.

Turning to see who could be following her, she saw men in uniforms with Duke, Zelda and Tredmont, all breaking out into a run after her.

They couldn't stop her. Not when she was so close. Quickening her pace, she hopped over a fallen tree and burst through the bushes to see a set of six swans splashing at each other in the water. She gasped at the vision of her brothers playing and still together. None had been harmed. They would be a family again.

One of them began honking madly when she reached the sand of the small beach. All of them turned and began swimming toward her. One even took off flying to get to her faster. She retrieved a sweater when she was bit by a group of bugs and electricity surged through her body.

"What the hell are you doing?" Duke screamed.

Elsa's body convulsed and the taste of metal filled her mouth. Her teeth clamped as she dropped to her knees. The stings from the bugs made her back arch, but she pulled a second sweater out of her basket and threw it in the air.

Liam dive bombed to catch it over his head. He shifted before her eyes. The blond hair replaced the white feathers that had been there moments before. Arms replaced wings and soon, he dropped from the sky no longer able to take flight.

She gasped in horror as he rolled and landed at her knees.

"Elsa." He smiled up at her right as a second surge of electricity made her back arch and her body spasmed.

"She's wandering in the wilderness with a head injury," Duke explained hours earlier. His father blamed him. They shouldn't have left the hospital. She should have been restrained. Now it would cost thousands of dollars to get helicopters up and have police support. Duke didn't care. Take his inheritance. Take his college fund.

Take it all—just help him find his lost girl.

"We have a visual," a voice crackled over the officer in front of Duke's radio. *"Turn left and go through to a small body of water about five hundred feet away. It's an open area. I can see a woman fitting the description on the edge of the water."*

Duke took off in a full sprint with his father, Zelda and a handful of police at his side. There seemed to be a wall of bushes that had been pushed aside. He crawled through the small opening and saw his lost girl with her basket of sweaters on her arm.

Right as he was going to call out, Zelda grabbed a taser from the hip of the officer that had his hands up and had been calling to the lost girl. Barbs connected to live wires shot from the gun and speared his girl's back.

She shook and convulsed.

"What the hell are you doing?" he cried out as he slapped the gun from Zelda's hand.

It cracked when it hit the ground and he watched his lost girl toss a sweater up in the air. The next thing he couldn't explain and wondered if the delusion was his alone. A swan dove into a sweater and a teenager with blond curls emerged through the head of the sweater.

"Elsa," the boy cried as he rolled and came to rest at her knees.

Elsa? Was that his lost girl's name? A second round of electricity must have sparked through her as she shook, but still tossed another sweater. The swans on the pond that should have taken flight when the humans arrived were coming toward the shore. His lost girl continued to toss the sweaters that had scarred her hands. Swans honked and waved their wings to keep people away as they ducked their heads inside the irritating fabric.

"What the fuck?" an officer exclaimed as a group of six swans converted and changed into a set of young blond men.

Duke's skin rose as the noise went from animalistic calls, to a hard snapping like bones breaking. Or, they were reconfiguring to rid the boys of wings and webbed feet to arms and legs. They were naked, sans the sweaters, and appeared to be in their late teens to early twenties. Although less dirty, the men had striking features and reminded him of his lost girl. Blond, blue eyed and round faces on the younger men.

Every part of Duke searched for a reason. An explanation for the insanity before his eyes. People weren't able to shape shift. No costume was that good. And yet, before him were now six human males surrounding his lost girl in protection.

"Elsa," the boys cried.

She sat up on her knees. Weakened by the taser and her previous injuries as the boys pulled the barbs from her back all speaking at once, "Are you okay? Elsa, please say you're okay?"

Duke stared unsure what to do. When he saw her droop, he rushed to her side and pushed through the men wearing nothing but a set of nettle yarn sweaters. Catching her before she collapsed completely, he held his lost girl in his arms.

She took in the vision of the men around her and reached her hand up to his face. "Hey you," she said with a melodic voice and tears streaming from her eyes back into her blonde curls. "I'm Elsa, Elsa Swanson."

He ran his fingers through her hair as he sat down and pulled her on his lap. Bringing his forehead to hers, he laid a delicate kiss to her lips. Now he was the one unable to speak. *Elsa.* His lost girl was no longer lost. She had been living on the land her father owned.

"I'm Elsa," she repeated. "And I'm in love with you Duke King."

"Your voice is the most beautiful thing I've ever heard in my life."

"Zelda is a witch. Please don't think I'm crazy, but she is. You saw my brothers. She changed them into swans. If I made a sound, they would have died."

"All the times she hurt you, she was trying to kill them?"

"Yes."

Duke turned to his father who's arms were crossed. He couldn't deny what she was saying. Magic existed in the world. They had all seen the swans shift into a new form.

"Arrest her," Duke ordered the officer.

"For what?" he asked. "I can't exactly book her for witch craft."

"Witchcraft?" Zelda pishawed. "Truly. You are all mentally unstable."

"I can book her for discharging my weapon," the officer offered. "It's only a few days, but it is something."

"Fine," Tredmont said. "I'll be drawing up fraud charges. You knew this girl was the rightful owner of the property you were trying to sell me."

"I had no idea who she was."

"That's why you were constantly hurting her," Duke accused. "You have medical support as part of this search right?"

"Yes." The officer used his radio to get a helicopter to land in a clearing.

"Elsa," Duke began enjoying the feel of her name on his lips. "You're going to the hospital and you are staying until the doctor says you are healthy enough to leave."

"Will you be my doctor?"

"No," he said and her face dropped a little bit. "I will be your fiancé and your husband the moment you are released."

Elsa's body had to be flushed of toxins. Duke helped apply the bandages to the cuts in her back from the taser. Thankfully, the sweatshirt she had been wearing cut down the impact, but it still hurt her. The concussion she had been told would be an issue for a few weeks or months. Duke didn't seem to mind the broken and battered woman he pledged himself to.

"Are you ready to get out of this place?" Bjorn asked as he rolled a wheelchair into the room.

Now in his twenties, he was poised to take their father's place in the business as he slowly learned the ropes. All of them would be getting private tutors to help them catch up with their studies.

"We've cleaned up our old home," Liam said. "Mr. King said he'd take it off our hands."

"Maybe I want to live there with Duke," she said thinking it was the perfect home for children.

"Don't you want to live in father's home?" Taghe asked.

The hospital room seemed smaller than the last time she was here. A group of wild boys all here to care for her, but it was the man who pushed past them and came to help her off the bed she wanted by her side.

"I heard there was a lot of noise disrupting other patients on the ward."

"You have no idea how loud we can get," Elsa teased. "The Swanson's are a wild bunch. What do you expect from a group of kids raised by each other?"

"I'm just happy your voice is one of the bunch. Come show me this mansion you own. I have to decide if you're rich enough for me to marry."

"It only seems fitting that a princess marry a king don't you agree?" she said and leaned her forehead on his.

The authorities didn't know how to deal with a witch turning six boys into swans. Duke admitted if she had the ability to talk and would have explained it to him. He would have let Zelda lock her away. Little did the witch know, her punishing dictates of silence on the curse saved Elsa in the end and brought her closer to Duke. He would be her king. He would be her heart. If witches still existed in the world, then so could fairytales and that meant Elsa had earned her happily ever after.

The End

READ ALL **15** BOOKS THAT ARE PART OF THE F'd UP

FAIRY TALES

COLLECTION FIND OUT MORE ABOUT THE COLLECTION

HERE

WARNING These are NOT the stories your mama told you.

1. RED- KASSANNA DWIGHT
2. THE CINDERELLA PLAN- DIANE FLAME
3. FEELING FROGGY- ANALISE NIXON
4. ALICE IN MOVIE LAND- EDEN ROYCE
5. THE PRINCESS BED- LAVERNE THOMPSON
6. LA BELLE BETE- DAHLIA WINTERS
7. THE MUTED SWAN- MICHEL PRINCE
8. DO NO CHARM- JAYHA LEIGH & JEANIE JOHNSON
9. FOR YOU, I QUILL- LEELA LOU DAHLIN
10. FLAWLESS- REANA MALORI
11. SLEEP SWEETLY- ANGEL MYSTIQUE
12. SNOW- TAIGE CRENSHAW & MCKENNA JEFFERIES
13. GOLDEN REPUNZELS- DEIDRA DS GREEN & STEPHANIE N BREWER
14. INTO THE DARKNESS- SIREN ALLEN
15.

ABOUT THE AUTHOR

Michel Prince is an author who graduated with a bachelor degree in History and Political Science. Michel writes new adult and adult paranormal romance as well as contemporary romance.

With characters yelling, "It's my turn damn it!" She tries to explain to them that alas, she can only type a hundred and twenty words a minute and they will have wait their turn. She knows eventually they find their way out of her head and to her fingertips and she looks forward to sharing them with you.

When Michel can suppress the voices in her head, she can be found at a scouting event or cheering for her son in a variety of sports. She would like to thank her family for always being in her corner and especially her husband for supporting her every dream and never letting her give up.

Michel has been awarded Elite Status with Rebel Ink Press in 2013, the service award for her local RWA chapter Midwest Fiction Writers in 2013 and 2014 and is a Pro member of RWA. She lives in the Twin Cities with her husband, son, and dog Bolt.

You can follow Michel on Facebook, Twitter or at her website.

OTHER BOOKS BY MICHEL PRINCE

First And Ten Book One Love By The Yard Series

In Chicago they say Speed Kills, or at least they have for the last seven years since the handsome running back, Jerome Speed, led the Chicago Grizzlies to divisional and conference championships.

Danika Albright's privileged upbringing has most people believing she wants for nothing. As the daughter of a self-made billionaire she shouldn't, but her father never wanted his children to be spoiled and demanded they make their own way with little to no help from him. While working her way through school as a stylist, she crosses paths with a local football star with his own issues.

The pair work to keep their desires from molding their relationship, but when a paternity case tackles the star and the woman wants more than money, the relationship takes a hit.
Can Danika and Jerome look past what they know and take the time to discover what really happens when you fall in love with a person—one who wants you and not just your name?

Two people—two different backgrounds—one goal—to learn to love one yard at a time.

Second and Short Book Two Love by the Yard Series

Offensive linemen are considered the silent protectors of the game. Always expected to be there, but never seen by the fans. Whether by accident or circumstance, Dalton Gresham has been known as the Blood Thirsty Bear of the Gridiron since his rookie year. With fans wearing number seventy-seven with fake blood dripped on it, can this giant in football shake his monster status?

Having hidden away at Lost Lake, Wisconsin, the last thing Willeen Fire needed was publicity. The tall, voluptuous woman has a beauty she hides behind flannel shirts and engine grease while staying off the grid. When Dalton first meets Willeen, the last thing he thought was she was a woman in need of protection. But as he falls for her, the natural instinct to protect is screaming in his ears.

Can Dalton stop being the monster he's been labeled and become the one who will finally save Willeen from the man hunting her?

Third and Long Book Three Love by the Yard Series

Ten years ago, Coach Xavier Jackson was poised to complete a lifelong journey. When he wasn't picked up after the seventh round of the draft was over, he was left to wonder if his dreams of playing professional football were finally over. Instead, with a chance as a free agent he made good on his, but the lure of off-field activities led the tight end to make the worst decision of his life.

Chelsea Monroe was engaged to the best football player their little college had ever seen. She'd become part of his family, tasked with keeping his baby sister, Leeda, safe when he had to go away. But a visit between training put an end to everything, leaving her shattered and unwilling to give herself to anyone ever again.

Though a decade of focus on her career made her a sought after litigator, it kept her from making any personal connections. Chelsea decides to take a trip to Jamaica before her fresh start in Chicago, but instead of it being a break, it turns into a second chance.

Leeda Jackson has plans for her brother and the woman that should have been her sister.

Unwrapping A Marriage

Co-authored with Reana Malori

What do you do when the love that once set you free, feels like it's holding you prisoner?

Sterling and Elizabeth Jackson have built a life most would envy. A beautiful home, two wonderful children and a very comfortable lifestyle. Yet something is tearing them apart. With divorce looming, they are trying to make it through the holiday season for their family.

With clashing schedules, demands from employers and two busy kids, the former lovers have managed to stay out of each other's orbit, at least for a while. But Fate, or maybe their well-meaning family, has set them up on a collision course.

Past memories bubble up to the surface and there's nothing to stem the flow. What once was amazing has turned hurtful and full of pain. But is that the real story? Is it too late for a couple who once lived and breathed for each other to find their way back?

There's a thin line between love and hate. Will Sterling and Elizabeth be able to mend a love that seems broken and lost, or will the final pull on the holiday ribbon unwrap their last chance to save their marriage.

One Last Rodeo: A Red Hot and Boom! Story

Betsy Flynn's star is rising as she serves as the color sports reporter for the local CBS affiliate. Her focus, knowledge, and high heels have become a staple along every sideline in Minneapolis, but a rodeo has come to Minnesota and this Texas transplant will have to go back to her roots.

Five years ago, pick-up man JT Long chose his best friend's rodeo career over the love of his life, Betsy. As JT's rodeo shows up in Northern Minnesota, he quickly realizes his chances of winning Betsy back are getting slim as he learns he only has one last rodeo to win her heart.

*Break out the fireworks and get ready to kick off your summer with this HOT new collection of stories. One Last Rodeo is part of the Red Hot and BOOM multi-author series (stands alone for reading enjoyment)

One Last Sunset-Book One of the Long Ranch Series

Sunshine Parker didn't walk away from Tender Root, he ran. Joining the rodeo let his body be beaten by broncos for money, instead of his father for free. After an injury forces him to return to his hometown, he heads to the Long Ranch, the one place that's always accepted him.

Melody Long is Long Ranch's first cowgirl in a hundred years. With brothers and cousins always looming in the background, Melody had given up on dating long ago. Now back from college, she uncovers something even the Long name can't protect her from.

Men who want to survive keep Melody at arm's length. But Melody isn't the bookworm Sunshine remembers growing up, and it's hard to hide his new found lust. Will his desire cost him the only place he's ever considered home?

The Last To Know-Book Two of the Long Ranch Series

Savannah Georgio stopped wondering about who her father was before she turned eight. Her mother made it clear she would never tell. So, why worry about someone who would never be there? Only someone did know about her and soon, she was on her way to Tender Root, New Mexico to inherit land from a man she never knew.

Clayton Long was raised with the belief he would one day not only work, but own the Long Ranch. As he got older, he saw he wasn't the heir, but the spare to the ranch as his older brothers and cousins blocked him from major decisions. When the Winston Bastard showed up in town, his brother taps him for a special project to save the ranch. Only Clayton gets distracted because when he looks at Savannah, he sees a future with the girl trying to discover who she is.

As secrets get revealed and family members question the validity of Savannah's claim, she can only count on one man from the neighboring ranch, but is he too, keeping a secret that will have her running from her new family?

The Last Laugh Book Three of the Long Ranch Series

In Tender Root, New Mexico, Montgomery Long seemed singularly focused on fun. The middle child he only had one real duty, taking care of his younger sister Melody. But he'd failed and as the months tick on without her attacker behind bars he's itching to exact revenge on the man who almost took his baby sister's life.

Harper Maxwell's year had gone from bad, to worse. With an ex husband looming around making her life miserable, the chance to get away to Mexico for a case made sense. As the attorney assigned to the Long case she was set to serve extradition paperwork and hopefully catch a few rays at the beach before heading back home.

If only that could have happened, with threats on Harper's life can she find safety or even love in the arms of a man who never commits and worse yet may only be a rebound? Or will she become the next tragedy that could destroy the Long Ranch?

At Long Last Book Four of the Long Ranch Series

When gunshots echoed outside the courthouse in Las Cruces, New Mexico, Miles Long took off in a blind rage of protection. Two men were dead and Miles and his family were the ones in handcuffs. Quiet and reserved, the bookworm cowboy has to keep from being locked up and save the ranch, his family worked for over a century.

Ashleigh Wood had one job, help Hamilton Boyle convict three members of the Long family for murder. Being against her best friend's new family and tasked with researching the history of the Longs, she soon discovers she's falling in love the man whose bullet matches the fatal shot.

Can Ashleigh set aside the desire drawing her to a man she knows is capable of murder? Will justice finally come to the Longs' of Tender Root, or will the final straw destroy what their family has struggled to build?

The Guardian's Heart-Book One of the Growing Strong Series

Nominated for Book of the Year 2013 By LASR
Case Thomas is always in control whether it's on the basketball court, the lab where he works, or in his love life. He thinks he has everything all figured out. All that changes when his parents pass away during his last year of college and Case is thrown into fatherhood when he becomes temporary guardian to two adorable twin toddlers. Weeks later, exhausted and running out of time, Case must decide if he's ready to become a father to these children, or give them up and move on with what's left of his life. Then he meets Gabbie Vaulst.

Gabbie is amazing with the kids, owns her own business, and has all the right curves in all the right places. She can tell Case is attracted to her, but does he really love her or is he just settling for a surrogate Mom who can wrangle his new kids? Knowing that she's falling in love with him, she chooses to push him away until his world straightens out. Can Case prove to Gabbie, and himself, that his feelings are real? Or, is this sudden family too much for both of them to handle?

The odds, as well as members of their past who've come out of the woodwork, are against them, but when kids are involved, all bets are off.

The Queen's Heart-Book Two of the Growing Strong Series

At the tender age of seventeen, Mary Beth discovered the family she thought would see her through anything couldn't accept her one mistake. Thank goodness for her best friends that stepped up to support her decision to keep her child. Seven years later together with her friends, she's created a successful business on the verge of a large expansion.

But the desire to be accepted by her family continues to be a failure that taints all her accomplishments and has her making concessions she never thought she would.

Elias Marquez was content with his life. He definitely wasn't looking for the vibrant redhead down the hall from him. After a chance encounter, he can't escape the need to be in her company again. He wants to explore the possibilities and the undeniable spark her touch inspires.

Torn between trying to right the past and accepting that she can only control her own life is Mary Beth truly ready for the love Elias is prepared to offer as a future?

The Politician's Heart-Book Three of the Growing Strong Series

Karen Schroeder made the choice to be a politician. Her local success has caught the eyes of her party and she's suddenly thrust into the national stage. She knows how to play the game and exactly who she needs to be, even if it's not who she really is.

Sarah Lindstrom has never questioned her feelings, even when they made her believe her girlfriend would say yes to her proposal instead of breaking up with her. When she sees Karen Schroeder campaigning, the rush of attraction is undeniable. Sarah knows she's been wrong before, but her feelings for Karen overwhelm any apprehension for this woman who's trapped in the closet.

As the relationship grows, Sarah learns love can be the painful when the one you love can only be herself with the door is closed. More importantly, her love of Karen could cost her everything she's worked for. Can love bloom when hidden in the dark?

The Teacher's Heart-Book Four in the Growing Strong Series

There's no way Amanda Butler would ever let herself get attached to anyone. Sure, sex is fun, but love is for suckers. Her parents taught her that. She has her friends, a job she loves, and lots of fun flings. Everything she thinks she wants.

Ashton Gilmore is at a crossroads when he meets Amanda. She's every thing he's ever wanted in a real relationship, but she might have too much baggage for even this hot political fixer handle.

For the past few years, the women of Growing Strong Montessori have been discovering loves they'd never thought possible. Sans one, Mandy who has spent the last few years taking one hit after another and can't see Ashton Gilmore as anything more than a bump in the road.

Ashton has to find a way to teach Mandy that love exists, before she gives up on the concept all together.

Silly Girl

Nominated for a RONE 2014
Are professional sports just children's games played by oversized kids?

With an all-consuming focus, Matthias Jessup has sacrificed his body in pursuit of greatness. But while he's enjoyed the spoils of being an elite athlete, the physical punishment can only be held at bay for so long. He knows his time is running out and he will have to face his future soon.

Sylvia Kinder is obsessed with Matthias' public image. But now, that her fantasy has walked into her life, could it possibly lead to a happy ending? She worries if there's any place for her in his world, much less his heart.

Drawn to each other on a chance meeting, Matthias must look off the court and discover the real world, while Sylvia will have to find the strength of self to not become lost in a world she doesn't understand. But those who aren't ready for a life after the game surround Matthias and are willing to do anything to keep him on the court.

Kiss from a Rose: A Red Hot Valentine Story

Jenna Turner wasn't looking for anything but a quick bite to eat when she met the sexy peace officer Marcus Peterson. While Jenna has always been singularly focused on her next big promotion at work, suddenly she's distracted by alluring texts from Marcus.

His evocative words and her naughty responses invoke emotions neither seem ready for, and luckily, neither have room in their busy lives to follow through on all their sexting.

Can two career driven people find the time to take their relationship to the next level? Or, will careers and the pressure to achieve goals cause the end to a budding love?

Mask of Fire: A Red Hot Treat

Barton Nuril has attended the Harvester's Gala for more years than most. He'd given up the dream that a woman would want him for more than copulation until a dark haired beauty he dubs Fire fights to get him in bed. Even as those from his province plot to take down the establishment and all its traditions, Barton for once, is discovering love may exist

Abigail Stone knew the Rules chapter and verse. Even as others perverted their purpose, Abby stayed true and attended the Harvester's Gala to find her soul mate. Just as she feels she's found him the fates step in between omens and a battle no one could have foretold Abby is sure her choice is doomed. Will she see beyond her traditions and still stay within the rules to find love?

Can love ignite when one believes it no longer exists and the other fears the fates have doomed the union?

Shared Redemption-Book One of the Frozen Series

Former slave Nye ended his life in 1859 after losing his love. The angel Gabriel has offered Nye a chance at redemption by hunting demons as a member of the Frozen. With less than seven years left until his salvation, Nye is staying on the straight and narrow – until a woman gets caught in the crossfire during a demon hunt.

After receiving devastating news, Kiriana Kladshon moves across the country, only to get caught up in the world of The Frozen. Nye and Kiriana are pulled into an attraction neither can control. Will it be their ultimate demise or their greatest salvation?

Damarion, is leading a group of female demons on a mission. During his punishment on Earth, Damarion learns of dangers within his coven trying to stop him from returning to his love, still trapped in Hell and A love he was so sure was true...

Redemption of Blood-Book Two of the Frozen Series

Trisha O'Driscoll started tending bar to give her a free schedule and quick cash. She never thought the young solider that wandered in with a fake ID would want a woman almost twenty-years-older. Although they drew the line at commitment, Trisha can't help falling for this mysterious stranger and his dark past.

James Schmitt took his life to escape his pain. The offer from Gabriel for salvation gave him a chance to take responsibility for his actions, but his inner demons won't stop tormenting him. Gabriel gave but one order—protect his partner Kiriana at any cost.

And he'll be damned if he lets anyone down ever again.

Princess LaDressa, daughter of Lucifer, has come for revenge on the woman who slew her beloved Damarion. Kiriana holds his ashes, and with them, his only chance for resurrection. One way or another, LaDressa will be united with her love.

Stolen Redemption-Book Three of the Frozen Series

Esther, Vincent, and Pivane thought they knew what side they were on.

When Esther became Frozen, she thought she'd spend the rest of her afterlife searching for salvation. She never thought she'd find it in the arms of a small town detective.

Vincent thought a small town would be just the place to bury his past. Mount Pleasant, Iowa is a sweet town on paper, the kind of town a guy could forget his feelings and live to serve and protect. He didn't count on meeting Esther and having the gates of his hearts forced open again.

With all his rivals captured or injured, Pivane is poised to finally become leader of his demon clan and make all his dreams come true. However, even his black heart can be touched by love. A love he'd have to throwaway everything for.

They thought they knew whose team they were on, but love changes everything.

Chrysalis-Book one of the Chrysalis Series

Winner of the Interracial Romance Author Expo Sweetest Romance 2015

In the annals of dysfunctional families, the Chisholm's are working their way to the top. Drug abuse, an unwed mother with multiple fathers, and the questionable cash flow for the 'pretty one'. All this from a seemingly normal, two parent middle class family. But were the choices truly made of their free will?

Bad choices are a Chisholm family trait, one that confounds the youngest child, Ellie, who's trying to separate herself by making smart decisions. And falling for Oscar Jeffreys, the hottest guy at school, would be number one on the list of Chisholm family disasters. Yet the crazy part is it's not a one sided attraction. Somehow, Ellie has caught Oscar Jeffreys' eye. Sure, she could see the barriers between them. Race, age, popularity. They were at opposite ends of the spectrum. But a demon set to destroy her family? She can't see that.

Oscar provides security and acceptance Ellie never imagined she deserved. As the passion of first love grows, Ellie honestly believes she has a chance to beat the odds and live a happy, normal life. Then her world collapses around her. With the help of a guardian angel, Ellie learns of a world that has unknowingly surrounded her for years. And she'll have to find strength buried deep inside to save not only her future, but flush out and stop the demon in her midst.

Ellie will have to learn that sometimes the hardest lesson about growing up is accepting that you're worth more.

The Beam-Book Two of the Chrysalis Series

When I was a child, I used to speak like a child, think like a child, reason like a child; when I became a man, I did away with childish things.-Corinthians 13:11

There comes a time in everyone's life when they must put aside their childish ways. In the past year, Ellie

Chisholm has fallen into the security of her relationship with Oscar Jeffreys, emerging with a stronger sense of herself. But now Ellie's mother has started inserting herself into Ellie's life, treating her as if she were a child even though Ellie has begun to make very adult decisions for her future. Having finally consummated her relationship with Oscar, Ellie learns the powers inside of her stretch further than vaporizing demons.

Maria, the demon bent on revenge, has been reigned in by God but that doesn't stop her from disrupting and threatening those around Ellie and Oscar. Ellie becomes off balance as Maria switches strategy and attempts to destroy Ellie from the outside. Now the gauntlet has been thrown down. Ellie must help her family achieve positive change and finally break the tie between her mother and Gaap or risk losing everyone she loves.

Can Ellie maintain her sanity while walking the last steps as a child?

Not Even Death Book Three of the Chrysalis Series

In one tragic moment, Ellie Jeffreys' perfect life ended and the devastation of losing the only man she believed she could ever love and their beautiful child causes the hopeless resignation that life shall never again be worth living. Bound by a decree from On High, the demons who tormented Ellie for years have had to leave the Jeffreys alone, but they grow restless, sensing Ellie's despair and vulnerability. They lust for her. And they're extremely resourceful.

Dr. Luke Page's inability to save Ellie's husband and son has him hoping to recover her crumbling mind and show her love does still exist in the world. Dr. Page feels immense pressure to be her security blanket in the concrete world, but thoroughly healing her presents a challenge that raises questions about his ability as both a physician and a human being. Ellie's depression now leaves her susceptible to the vengeful demons. In the past, the sheer strength of Oscar's love and devotion fortified a barrier around Ellie, shielding her from the effects of the world's iniquities.

Will Luke's love be enough to rise to the challenge of protecting her? Or will Oscar's become like a phoenix letting not even mortality stand its way?

Unto Us Book Four of the Chrysalis Series

No one ever said carrying demon spawn would be easy..." Ellie Jeffreys is unsure of when or where she woke up, but one thing is certain—she's not alone.

Having been violently ripped from her life, the return will be anything but smooth. Led back to the house and family she loves, Ellie soon learns an interloper will tie her to the enemy forever. Now unsure if the nightmare of Luke Page will consume her and finally allow Gaap to destroy the family she's created, she discovers the only way forward is to move on from the past and accept her place in an ancient prophecy.

Triple B Baking Co.-Book One of the Hearts of Braden Series

Three years ago a heart broken Merryn Sota got in a SUV and drove away from California. Call it fate or serendipity, but when the vehicle broke down outside of Braden, Iowa she fell in love with the calm and community. Using her skill as a baker she opened up Braden Buttery Bites Bakery which the town lovingly renamed the Triple B. Every confection she makes heals her wounded heart a little bit.

Ever since the tragedy, the only way Austin Larsen can cope with life is to have it completely regimented. The Triple B brought schedule to his life. Something to focus on day by day.

When a snowstorm hits the small town Austin's schedule is disrupted and old wounds are reopened.

Only the hospitality of the Triple B, along with Merryn, can right his world. However, as Merryn and Austin grow closer, their pasts resurface and threaten to destroy their happiness forever.

Hell Yeah! Hollywood Lights, Austin Nights
(Kindle World Novella) Book Nine of the Hearts of Braden Series.

Soren Birch wrote a movie deserving of the best Hollywood has to offer, but as a first time screenwriter, he's stuck on a shoestring budget. Vision Star has offered him a deal and set him up in Austin, Texas with Zane Saucier as a local contact. Now the actor turned writer will be donning a few hats, including director, as his passion piece comes to life.

In Hollywood, Alicia Winters' star is rising, but she is slowly learning quantity over quality after being kicked off her latest set. She then finds her way to her sister's bakery in Braden, Iowa. A few days of rest and little tough love has her ready to take a chance on a small budget film in Austin.

A dream actress and a company willing to take a chance on him, Soren is beginning to think he might actually make a name for himself beyond being a sex symbol. Can his luck finally be changing or will his attraction to Alicia derail his dream before it even starts?

<u>By the Light of Blizzard</u>

Kelsi Stamp is known all over the world as a best-selling science-fiction author. Living in a small town, she's able to stay hidden, tucked away in her cabin in the woods. Outside of her internet searches, she stays away from the world. Readers are fickle and love has turned to unhealthy obsession in the past. As a blizzard bears down on Northern Minnesota, Kelsi's lights flicker, then go out right after a large crash echoes through the wilderness.

A truck holds an unconscious stranger she is being pulled to, but who is Jace Runyon and why was he driving so fast on a road no GPS even knows exists?

Made in the USA
Lexington, KY
28 April 2017